UNIVERSITY OF NORTH CAROLINA AT CHAPEL HILL
DEPARTMENT OF ROMANCE LANGUAGES

NORTH CAROLINA STUDIES
IN THE ROMANCE LANGUAGES AND LITERATURES

ESSAYS; TEXTS, TEXTUAL STUDIES AND TRANSLATIONS; SYMPOSIA

Founder: URBAN TIGNER HOLMES

Distributed by:

UNIVERSITY OF NORTH CAROLINA PRESS
CHAPEL HILL
North Carolina 27514
U.S.A.

NORTH CAROLINA STUDIES IN THE
ROMANCE LANGUAGES AND LITERATURES
Texts, Textual Studies and Translations
Number 4

GIACOMO LEOPARDI

THE WAR OF THE MICE AND THE CRABS

GIACOMO LEOPARDI

THE WAR OF THE MICE
AND THE CRABS

Translated, introduced, and annotated by
ERNESTO G. CASERTA

CHAPEL HILL

NORTH CAROLINA STUDIES IN THE ROMANCE
LANGUAGES AND LITERATURES
U.N.C. DEPARTMENT OF ROMANCE LANGUAGES
1976

Library of Congress Cataloging in Publication Data

Leopardi, Giacomo, conte, 1798-1837.
　The war of the mice and the crabs.

　(North Carolina studies in the Romance languages and literatures. TTT; 4)
　Prose translation of Paralipomeni della Batracomiomachia.
　Bibliography: p. 109.
　I. Caserta, Ernesto G., tr. II. Title. III. Series: North Carolina studies in the Romance languages and literatures. Texts, textual studies, and translations; 4.

PQ4709.E5P4 1974　　　　　853'.7　　　　　74-23182

ISBN 9780807891643

DEPÓSITO LEGAL: V. 289 - 1976

ARTES GRÁFICAS SOLER, S. A. - JÁVEA, 28 - VALENCIA (8) - 1976

A mia moglie, Jane,
affettuosa compagna di viaggio

TABLE OF CONTENTS

FOREWORD

Giacomo Leopardi (Recanati, 1798-1837, Naples) has few peers among European poets of the nineteenth century and in Italian literature he stands with Dante, Petrarch, Ariosto, Tasso, and Manzoni, yet outside an elite group of specialists his art is still little known in the English speaking world. In recent years the Canti *and some of the prose works have reached a wider audience through the translations and essays of such scholars as Cecchetti, Singh, and Whitfield. The present translation, born of a genuine admiration for the poet and a long familiarity with his poetry, is a further contribution to these efforts to render Leopardi's artistic personality less vague, less amorphous in the minds of those who, for lack of knowledge of Italian, have read only a few of his works.*

My free translation of the erudite sounding title (Paralipomena of the Batrachomyomachia would mean "Additions" to the Batrachomyomachia *of Homer) is in part an attempt to lead the contemporary reader into a vital and even timely work of art, a satire on war and balance of power in a world ruled only by expediency, where the strong, under the pretext of affording protection to the weak, exercise their power with the utmost arrogance. Fundamentally a work of political satire,* The War of the Mice and the Crabs *is a humorous, ironic, and often surprisingly lyric tale. Never before published in English translation, it is Leopardi's longest, most controversial, and perhaps most misunderstood work.*

The translation is based on the standard critical edition of F. Moroncini, Opere minori, approvate di Giacomo Leopardi, *Vol. I:* Poesie *(Bologna: Licinio Cappelli, 1931). I have also consulted F. Flora's edition of* Tutte le opere di Giacomo Leopardi *(Milan: Mondadori, 1940), Vol. I, as well as the edition of A. Donati, published in the "Scrittori d'Italia" series by Laterza (Bari, 1921), and the editions prepared by E. Allodoli (Turin: UTET, 1927) and S. Solmi,* Giacomo Leopardi, Opere, Tomo I *(Milan-Naples: Ricciardi, 1956).*

My prose translation follows the Italian text as closely as possible. In many cases, however, due to the poet's classical syntax and to numerous convoluted constructions necessitated by rhyme, I have reconstructed entire sentences and sometimes entire octaves in order to render the meaning clear.

I wish to express my sincere gratitude to Professor Giovanni Cecchetti, who introduced me to the study of the Paralipomeni, *and to my wife, Jane, who collaborated with me on this work.*

INTRODUCTION *

The *Paralipomeni della Batracomiomachia* is Giacomo Leopardi's longest poem. Composed after the *Canti* and the *Operette morali*, between 1830 and 1837, and for the most part during his residence in Naples, the work was first published in Paris in 1842, but until recent years it has enjoyed little favor among scholars due to various prejudices both moral and aesthetic. Most of the opinions expressed about the poem during the second half of the nineteenth century and the first part of the twentieth are, in fact, based on reservations of a political and pedagogical nature. They often reflect the indignation of patriotic scholars who evaluated works of art from the standpoint of their possible moral, social, and political impact on the citizens.

Even the true admirers of Leopardi were shocked at the appearance of this work and could not help expressing surprise. Vincenzo Gioberti, for example, stated that Leopardi at the end of his life had written "un libro terribile," [1] and scarcely less vehement were the reactions of Giusti, Giordani, and Capponi. The satire of the Italian Risorgimento was felt to be too ungenerous, especially by those who were so closely involved with the political destiny of Italy, and attempts were made to explain and justify it in consideration of the pessimism and personal suffering of the author.

As for the aesthetic prejudice, after the studies of De Sanctis critics continued to distinguish between two Leopardis: the pure

---

* This essay was originally published in *Italian Quarterly*, 66 (1973), pp. 3-23. It is reprinted here, in a slightly revised version, with the kind permission of the editors.
    [1] V. Gioberti, *Il geusita moderno* (Losanna: Bonamici, 1846-47), Vol. III, p. 484.

lyric poet, the singer of human unhappiness, and the moralist and skeptic who, misunderstood by his contemporaries, shut himself off in a desperate solitude. It was pointed out by several critics, including one of the greatest, Benedetto Croce,[2] that whenever he tried to leave his intimate world, his genuinely lyric vein, whenever he tried to laugh and to make others laugh, Leopardi was inferior to himself. Consequently it was recommended, in order to find the true and great Leopardi, to read his *Canti*, since elsewhere there was almost a desert of poetry or at best a few flowers.

On the basis of such a distinction, many works of Leopardi, including the *Operette morali* ("Moral Works") and the entire poetic production of the last period along with the *Paralipomeni* were sacrificed to silence. In recent years, however, thanks to a good number of young Italian scholars endowed with a new artistic sensitivity and provided with more penetrating and diversified critical instruments, even that other face of Leopardi's has been unveiled and proved to be no less attractive than the one already known. This general revaluation has included the *Paralipomeni,* which have received particular attention from Walter Binni[3] and especially from one of his followers, Gennaro Savarese.[4]

If in order to appreciate fully the *Paralipomeni* we must view the work in the larger context of Leopardi's whole literary production, it is no less important for the comprehension of the poem to be familiar with Leopardi's last period, since the poem is so closely related to the others composed in those years and so much a product of the same general poetic and ideological posture.

After the "Canto notturno di un pastore errante dell'Asia" ("Nocturne of a Wandering Shepherd in Asia"), written in 1830, we perceive a different tone in Leopardi's lyrics: a detachment from the myth of memories and illusions, a more frank, virile, and polemical attitude. Previously the contemplator of himself and

---

[2] B. Croce, *Poesia e non poesia,* 2nd ed. (Bari: Laterza, 1935), pp. 103-119.

[3] W. Binni, *La nuova poetica leopardiana,* 2nd ed. (Firenze: Sansoni, 1962).

[4] G. Savarese, *Saggio sui "Paralipomeni" di G. Leopardi* (Firenze: La Nuova Italia, 1967).

of nature, all concerned with finding and describing the roots of a miserable human destiny, Leopardi has become more aggressive, more sure of himself, more convinced of possessing the Truth and of the necessity of revealing it to his contemporaries, who for insincerity or for lack of courage to contemplate the human condition *en face* did not want to acknowledge "il Nulla eterno."

During his last stay in Recanati, after the disappointments experienced in Rome, Milan, Bologna, and Florence, he found his fellow-villagers no less unfriendly, vile, and arrogant than they had seemed to him when he was an adolescent. And beyond the mountains of his native village, in a new world where he had once hoped to find happiness, men were no better than those with whom he had grown up. They seemed to him presumptuous, conceited, over-confident in human progress and perfectibility, so positive that human destiny was secure in the hands of scientists and economists and that true wisdom, founded on statistics, could be discovered in various magazines and newspapers as well as in the books of philosophy and philology written in Germany. He, instead, had reached the conclusion that if the individual is unhappy, then society, which is made up of individuals, will never attain a new golden ege — which actually never existed except in the imagination of poets or in our own youthful dreams.

This new outlook on life resulted more directly from some personal experiences: the greater familiarity with which he was treated by a group of scholars (Vieusseux, De Sinner, Capponi, Colletta, Ranieri) during his last residence in Florence (1830-33) and his unrequited love for Fanny Targioni-Tozzetti, which, after rejuvenating his heart and restoring his hopes, had the effect — after her rejection — of deepening his understanding and strengthening his character.

The pessimistic attitude dominant in the earlier poetry turned to irony and satire. Rather than lament his own unhappiness, Leopardi tried to laugh at men whom he knew to be sad even while they hypocritically declared the contrary. In the "Dialogo di Tristano e di un amico" ("Dialogue between Tristan and a Friend") he declared:

> I believed that my mourning voices, since evils are common, would be repeated in the heart of every listener.

But when I found out that people were not denying some particular statements but the whole matter and saying that life is not sad, and that if it looked to me this way it had to be out of an affect of sickness or of some other particular misfortune of mine, at first I remained astonished, bewildered, as still as a rock, and for many days I thought that I was in another world; afterwards, when I came to myself, I became a bit angry; finally I laughed. [5]

In this period the poet shifted his attention to society in order to reveal to his contemporaries their hypocrisy and fatuity. He felt that they were for the most part children who wanted to act like adults and that he was one of the few real men left, who out of shame had to hide themselves, just as someone who walks straight would feel compelled to do in a town of lame persons.

From his disappointment in love were born poems like "Il pensiero dominante" ("Sovereign Thought"), "Amore e Morte" ("Love and Death"), "A se stesso" ("To Himself"), and "Aspasia," while from this new attitude towards society and the culture of his time derived a series of ironic and satiric poems, the "Palinodia al marchese Gino Cappini," "I nuovi credenti" ("The New Believers"), "La ginestra" ("The Broom"), and the *Paralipomeni*. During this same period Leopardi wrote the *Pensieri*, which express a human experience of rare moral height and which may serve as an introduction and commentary to the *Paralipomeni*.

Leopardi was acquainted with some of the leading Italian cultural milieux: in Florence he was close to the group which, headed by Vieusseux, expressed their progressive views in the *Antologia*, and in Naples, through Antonio Ranieri, he met another enthusiastic group of intellectuals, including Galluppi, Troya, Pilla, Tari, and Ruggiero, all of whom professed spiritualistic and idealistic beliefs. Leopardi, instead, remained faithful to the materialistic philosophy of the Enlightenment, which in the *Paralipomeni* he celebrates with true nostalgia, covering with ridicule all optimistic and idealistic thinkers. That is why Leccafondi (Bottom-Licker), a fanatic admirer of German philosophy and

---

[5] All translations are mine. On this dialogue, cf. G. Cecchetti, "Il 'Tristano' di G. Leopardi, *Belfagor* (marzo 1964), pp. 131-140.

learning, is ironically called Signor di Pesafumo and Stacciavento (Lord of Smoke-Weigher and Wind-Sifter).

The irony which Leopardi directs at the Carbonari and their political conspiracies, on the other hand, finds added justification in the fact that many other Italian scholars of sincere patriotic sentiment reacted negatively to the ill-fated movements of 1820-21. Among them were Giovita Scalvini, Gino Capponi, Cattaneo, Giusti, and Manzoni himself, who believed that the salvation of the Italians lay in a gradual spiritual and moral change, not in violence and revolution.

In Naples even more than in Florence Leopardi was annoyed by the ineptitude of these optimistic intellectuals. His philosophy was disliked by lay and religious scholars alike, and the hymns of Terenzio Mamiani were preferred to his poetry. He reacted against the Neapolitan intellectual circles with "I nuovi credenti" just as he had written the "Palinodia" in answer to the Florentine scholars. However, he felt that these poems were not sufficient to express his complete disdain for this cultural world and wanted to compose the longer and more complex *Paralipomeni*, in which he would reorchestrate in a new imaginative composition the various polemic and satiric motives of the earlier works, including many of the *Operette* (e.g., "Dialogo della Terra e della Luna" and "Dialogo d'Ercole e di Atlante," etc.). In the *Operette*, however, the satire is contained in the veil of the fable, whereas in the *Paralipomeni* it is open and more direct. And as the first *operetta*, the "Storia del genere umano" ("History of Mankind"), is a prelude to the various poetic motives of the *Operette morali* and at the same time a synthesis of the poet's activity in this period, [6] so the *Paralipomeni* is the work which synthesizes the various poetic themes of Leopardi's last period.

Leopardi confessed his total disillusionment in the "Tristano," saying that he was willing to accept death more readily than the fame of Alexander and Caesar cleansed of all stain. The poetry of this period is less a struggle against Nature and human destiny than a protest against the foolish world, the error in which the men of his time liked to live. Its strong polemic tone is accom-

---

[6] Cf. G. Cecchetti, "Il Leopardi della 'Storia del genere umano'," in *Leopardi e Verga* (Firenze, 1962), pp. 3-44.

panied by a deep sense of compassion and sustained by a secret hope that the satire will not be altogether fruitless. Leopardi's laughter is rarely bitter or sarcastic and is often mixed with sadness, since the poet's irony derives not from a totally nihilistic view of mankind but from disesteem of those who would follow their own selfish ends instead of working with others to extirpate the evils within themselves and outside in the world.

In "La ginestra" he contrasts the general euphoria of his contemporaries with the nothingness of man living under the constant threat of Nature: the lava of Vesuvius is a visible reminder of our ephemeral existence, yet man continues to defy time with tricks and lies:

> Here gaze, here look at yourself,
> Proud and foolish century,
> You who abandoned the path
> Renascent thought marked forward to our days,
> Turning your steps backward,
> Boasting your regress,
> Calling your failure advance!
> . . . . But I
> Shall not go down to the grave bearing such shame;
> I will release the scorn that flares
> For you in my heart as openly as possible, although
> I know how history
> Crowds out those who over-offend their age.
>
> (lines 51-69)

Leopardi called his poem the "Paralipomena" ("Additions") of the *Batrachomyomachia* apparently because he wanted to continue the narration of the battle between the frogs and the mice of the homonymous pseudo-Homeric poem, *Batrachomyomachia*, which he had translated into Italian three times (1816, 1821, 1826). His poem, in fact, starts just where the Homeric poem ends, with the defeat of the mice caused by the intervention of the crabs, sent by Jupiter, who along with the other gods did not want the total extermination of the frogs. Leopardi relates this futile battle of mice, frogs, and crabs to the revolutionary movements of the Italians (especially those which took place in 1820-21 and in 1830-31) against the Austrians. The Italians would be the poor mice defeated by the crabs, the Austrians, described in their brutal strength and rough manners.

Besides the pseudo-Homeric *Batrachomyomachia,* which was undoubtedly a primary source and at the same time a model to emulate, Leopardi may have had in mind the *Animali parlanti* of Giambattista Casti and, in the opinion of some critics (e.g., Moroncini), Byron's *Don Juan* or *The Age of Bronze,* which is full of political allusions. The Dog, the liberal minister of the king in the *Animali parlanti,* looks like Leccafondi (Bottom-Licker) in the *Paralipomeni,* and in both works the government, the populace, and the intrigues and cunning of the courtiers are ridiculed. In both works we find two stanzas in which virtue is exalted, the description of the prehistoric world and references to the legendary island of Atlantis, as well as the abrupt end of the narration with the pretext of the loss of the manuscript.

The *Paralipomeni* have in common with *Don Juan* the contempt for despotism (an attitude which Leopardi inherited more directly from the theater of Alfieri and from the patriotic poetry of the early Risorgimento), several digressions on philosophical, religious, and moral issues, and especially the disdain for newspapers, statistics, and political economy. In addition, the episode of the heroic deaths of the old Turk and his children before the victorious enemy is very similar to the heroic death of Rubatocchi (Chunk-Stealer). But these similarities are extrinsic and we know that the personality of Leopardi has very little in common with Byron's.

On the other hand, Leopardi knew so well the works of the ancient, medieval, and Renaissance fabulists that it would be impossible to determine precisely which sources, if any, were directly influential. Leopardi was a friend of Pietro Colletta and so me may assume that he was familiar with Colletta's *History of the Kingdom of Naples,* but even with respect to historic documents we wander in the dark since the poet may have gotten his material directly from the chronicles and newspapers of his day or from oral sources. In some characters, like Boccaferrata (Ironed-Mouth) and Camminatorto (Crooked-Walker), we find the same spirit that animated a number of contemporary journals, such as the *Voce della verità* and the *Voce della ragione.* * It must

---

* This periodical, founded and published in Pesaro, was run almost single-handedly by Leopardi's father, Monaldo, who was also an assiduous

be borne in mind that a work of art, if it is truly so, is always original and that critics who focus their attention exclusively on its sources miss their primary function. Therefore, we leave the ascertainment of facts and the verification of doubts to other scholars, in order to take a closer look at the content and significance of the *Paralipomeni*.

The poem begins with the bloody flight of the mice, put to rout by the frogs after the intervention of the crabs. The retreat of the mice reminds the poet of recent historical events: of the flight of the papal army led by General Colli during the Napoleonic War, and the retreat of the Belgians after defeat in 1831. In their desperate flight, the mice dare not look back until, suddenly, Miratondo (Looker-Around) stops, stands upright, looks all around, and ventures to inform his companions that there is not a crab in sight.

In the silence of the night the mice regain confidence and elect a new chief, Rubatocchi (Chunk-Stealer). The poet contrasts the fatuity of these false heroes with the valor of the ancient Roman soldiers; he mourns Italy's past glory and bemoans her present state of decadence.

Under the leadership of Rubatocchi the mice elect a messenger to the crab camp. Their unanimous choice is Leccafondi (Count Bottom-Licker), well known for his patriotism and liberalism, enlightened, in possession of an encyclopedic culture, optimistic, a typical "nuovo credente." After a short rest, the count along with a small company of servants, fully confident in the success of the mission, begins his journey by moonlight along a solitary road.

As Canto II begins, the count hastens his steps and, on the alert for danger, rejoices at the song of the cuckoo, undoubtedly a good omen. He feels himself to be a new Ulysses, but on drawing closer to the enemy camp he begins to tremble and would even turn his back and flee were it not for his aristocratic sense of honor. Having raised the olive branch, he leads his party into the crab camp, his teeth chattering. The crabs rush upon them, and would devour them all except that they see the count wearing glasses and speaking their language perfectly.

---

contributor to the other reactionary paper, *La voce della verità*, published in Modena.

The mice are tied up and brought before Brancaforte (General Strong-Claw), who, as soon as he hears the liberal count speaking of people, votes, and elections, not only does not want to recognize the new government of the mice and the count as their ambassador, but puts the count and his party in jail. After the intervention of Senzacapo (Emperor Without-Head) in favor of the unfortunate prisoners, Leccafondi (Count Bottom-Lincker) is permitted to stand before Brancaforte, who spitting frequently and in a very arrogant manner presents the theory of the European balance of power formulated after the final defeat of Bonaparte at the Congress of Vienna and reinforced with the Holy Alliance. In brief, he says that the crabs are the policemen of Europe and that they derive this privilege from their strength and their hard shell.

The pact is drawn up: the mice will have to lodge thirty thousand crabs and give them plenty of food and drink and double pay for a certain number of years. The count agrees, on condition that his government approves of the terms, and, happy at the thought of the truce, he starts back to his camp. On leaving, he encounters a few old frog acquaintances who, when asked how they are getting along under the dominion of the crabs, lament their miserable state, and the count concludes that the plight of the mice is not so bad after all.

In Canto III Rubatocchi (Chunk-Stealer) leads his army back home to Rat City, which is built entirely underground and whose only sign of life is the great stench issuing from its holes. The mice regain their customary self-confidence: they start anew to read newspapers and to speak of patriotism in the piazzas and cafés while they anxiously await the return of the count.

But Rubatocchi unexpectedly refuses the offer of the kingdom and the poor mice have to hold another election. They decide to restore the monarchy, which will be tempered by a constitution. The candidate is Rodipane (Bread-Muncher), who on account of his marriage to the daughter of the late king, Mangiaprosciutti (Ham-Eater), possesses all of the royal qualifications for the throne. Elected by popular support, Rodipane gives free cheese and polenta to the people and promises to defend by all means the constitution.

In Canto IV the poet explains why the customs and behavior of the mice, who lived in very ancient times, seem so much like ours today. The answer, he says, is given by those modern thinkers who maintain that the present civilized state of mankind must still be called primitive. Leopardi laughs at the theoreticians who believe in a golden age from which man has fallen either for having sinned against God, as the Christian tradition has taught and as Lamennais and De Maistre were then confirming, or on account of the corruption inherent to the process of civilization itself, as Rousseau affirmed. The poet debates whether the city came before the citizen or the citizen before the city, criticizing all reasoning founded on premises accepted *a priori* as well as the theory of innate ideas.

Meanwhile the mice, who reason somewhat like men, are convinced that their misery is the result of their own corruption, since Nature is always kind to her children. Some refugees, thinking of their country, shed tears of sorrow, while those at home crown their generous king, Rodipane (Bread-Muncher), who henceforth will be called king of the mice and not king of Rat City, and Rodipane I instead of Rodipane IV.

While the celebrations are still going on, Leccafondi returns to report the conditions of the truce demanded by the enemy, which at first seem dishonorable and unfair, but overcome by their desire for peace the mice agree to everything. The count undertakes a second journey to the camp of the crabs, who, as soon as they get the news, descend like a flock of vultures on Rat City. Leccafondi is loaded with honors for his diplomatic success and, elected Secretary of the Interior, he opens new schools, establishes new chairs in the colleges, and stimulates industry and trade. The new boom in industry is reflected in the construction of theaters, gymnasiums, and public buildings. But the crabs become suspicious of such progress and Senzacapo (Emperor Without-Head) decides to dispatch an envoy to the court of the mice.

Canto V begins with the speech of Boccaferrata (Ironed-Mouth), who, exposing the necessity of legitimate successions, says in substance that Senzacapo orders the abrogation of the constitution and prohibits popular participation in the government and that only on these conditions will the kingdom of the mice and their king be recognized by the crabs. Rodipane would very willingly consent to do without the constitution, but the mice are determined to defend it with their lives. War is declared and everywhere patriotic songs are heard. Rubatocchi (Chunk-Stealer), like the great Achilles, in the moment of danger puts aside his pride and assumes the command and the destiny of the mice. But even before the two armies clash, the mice, forgetting the eloquent orations of the piazzas, panic and flee through the hills, just as they had done before. Only Rubatocchi remains on the field, crushing enemy heads with his Herculean club. At sunset, exhausted from fighting the entire crab army, he falls, and the poet is stirred by such heroism to praise valor, no less noble when displayed by a mouse.

In Canto VI, Brancaforte (Strong-Claw) seizes Rat City, which capitulates thanks to those crabs who were already inside the walls. The city is pillaged and put under martial law, every sign of freedom is banished, the constitution is abrogated, and whoever speaks of such things is put in jail. Leccafondi is discharged. Rodipane is kept as a puppet king, while Camminatorto (Crooked-Walker) has the power of a dictator. The schools, factories, and theaters are all shut down. The ignorance and the arrogance of the occupation army reigns everywhere, yet the mice don't give up: after a period of silence, they start again to show signs of boldness, they read newspapers, they grow mustaches and sideburns, and at night they sing patriotic hymns. Camminatorto easily discovers that the real promoter of this revival of patriotism is Leccafondi and without any hesitation sends him into exile. The count starts to wander from court to court, imploring help for himself and his poor mice. One evening he is caught in a storm and almost drowns. In the darkness he sees a faraway flickering light and after much difficulty is ushered into a magnificent palace where he is sheltered by its solitary master, Daedalus, a man who prefers animals to his fellow men. The count is treated to a royal dinner of dried figs, Parmesan cheese, and milk, after which, like Aeneas at the request of Dido, he begins the narration of his adventures.

In the last two cantos (VII and VIII), which form the second part of the poem, Leccafondi and Daedalus journey to Atlantis and descend into Hell to consult the dead souls of the mice in order to find a solution to the problems of the mouse race. Daedalus serves as guide and teacher to his companion, as Virgil did for Dante. He has a vast experience of the world, of which he seems weary, but he is unable to help the count liberate his people. The count must go alone into the underworld of the mice while Daedalus waits for him outside, since the hole is too narrow for his human form. The count meets many heroes of the past, among whom Mangiaprosciutti and Rubatocchi, and asks them whether the regeneration and liberation of the mice is near and whether it will be brought about by the foreign support promised him. The whole underworld resounds with their laughter, burying the hopes of the count and of all liberal mice. Disheartened, the count reattaches his pair of wings and in the company of Daedalus flies back to Rat City, where, following the advice of the shades, he immediately consults Assaggiatore (General Taster). After much evasion the wise general is on the point of speaking when the poet says that, for lack of documents, he is unable to complete the narration.

Externally the *Paralipomeni* are a political satire of the Carbonari and in particular of the Neapolitan patriots, always optimistic when they were in the piazzas and open-air cafés but ready to run at the first sight of the enemy. However, the scope of the satire is much broader, including not only the Austrians (the crabs), described as barbarians, and Hegelian idealism, but the entire cultural trend of the century. To Leopardi the Italians seemed ridiculous in the way they carried out their conspiracies, with their superficial manifestations of warlike fierceness (thick mustaches and long sideburns), with their oratory and self-exaltation, because they fled at the very appearance of the dust raised by the marching enemy troops. They were daydreamers because they were hoping to receive foreign military assistance and did not realize that unless they helped themselves, unless they stopped being children and became men, foreigners would not only have contempt for them but would be ready and willing to subjugate them.

Although the political satire constitutes the dominant motive of the *Paralipomeni* it is not the only one, and many critics, racking their brains to establish precise historical allusions beneath each character and event of the narration, have, on account of this unilateral reading, missed the real poetic significance of the work. It is not our intention here to document with exact historical references every incident of the war between the mice and the crabs because we are convinced that such precise documentation would be of little value in appreciating the poem. Let it suffice to say that the poet had in mind the Neapolitan revolution of 1820-21 and those which took place in Europe and Italy in 1830-31. In the flight of the mice, described in Canto I, we can recognize the defeat of Guglielmo Pepe at Androdoco, and the general himself in Rubatocchi (Chunk-Stealer), who leads the troops to safety; but some scholars have suggested other personalities, for example Joachim Murat, whose retreat after defeat by the Austrians at Tolentino (May 2 and 3, 1815) was well known to Leopardi, since pillaging occurred around his home town. Brancaforte (Strong-Claw) is commonly identified with Marshal Bianchi, who defeated Murat, while Camminatorto (Crooked-Walker) and Brancaforte (Ironed-Mouth) have suggested to many critics the name of the shrewd and cunning Metternich. Senzacapo (Without-Head) resembles a lot Emperor Francis I, who also liked to play the violin. Rodipane (Bread-Muncher) calls to mind King Ferdinand I of Naples, but Louis-Philippe has also been mentioned. Personifying the philosophy of history, optimism, and idealism, Daedalus may be identified with Jean-Jacques Rousseau or some German idealist. Assaggiatore (Taster), according to the most common interpretation, is the author himself.

More than a caricature of a limited group of political figures, however, Leopardi intended to give his answer to all the would-be heroes and false ideas of his time. Various historical personages are filtered through the poet's imagination and acquire their own particular identity within the poem. How ridiculous, in fact, the behavior of Leccafondi (Count Bottom-Licker)! We no longer think about the Prince of Canosa, Capponi, or Mazzini, but only about Leccafondi, the typical daydreamer, naive and superficial, as he was felt and portrayed by the poet.

Leopardi, who said that "the world is a league of scoundrels against true gentlemen, of cowards against generous people" (*Pensieri,* I), had no illusions concerning the success of the secret societies of the Risorgimento. There was always too great a discrepancy between what he wanted and what he thought to be historically feasible for him to hope for the social and political regeneration of mankind. Leopardi's unwavering skepticism and despair before the course of human events could not but give rise to the ironic overtones and the sense of the ridiculous which prevail in the *Paralipomeni.* The poet laughs at these new heroes who speak with so much eloquence and enthusiasm, who plan military strategies and social and political reforms from the balconies, yet face to face with the enemy tremble like leaves and flee like the wind. He ridicules all of the idealists and political visionaries who prefer to live in a dream and ignore the truth.

No one is spared the poet's ridicule, certainly not the journalists, who act like the prophets and benefactors of mankind with their predictions of progress and future prosperity, nor those who voraciously read such rubbish and base their lives upon it (I, 42). And not surprisingly the populace is the object of Leopardi's laughter, screaming like a herd, "Long live the Charter! Long live Bread-Muncher!" for the royal favor of some cheese and polenta (IV, 27).

The satirist launches out against the prominent political theorists of the time, who after the Restoration and the establishment of the Holy Alliance spoke of European balance of power and royal successions as if they were the executors of God's will, while in practice they resorted to the law of the jungle, using force in the most brutal manner against the helpless and poor nations. The satire is particularly virulent against the absolute power of the Austrians (the crabs), who with their strongly repressive methods destroyed all semblance of freedom and human dignity (VI, 6). More than once Leopardi expresses his great aversion to the Austrians, calling them "an army of greedy and strange brutes" (I, 13), "people without brains" (II, 39), and very often he alludes to their ignorance, saying that education and the arts "are not dear to those countries" (IV, 34).

Although Leopardi never explicitly formulated a political ideology, it can be said with certitude that he no longer adhered to the views of his father, Monaldo, the conservative author of the *Dialoghetti*, who favored the papal hegemony. He gives only marginal importance in the poem to the frogs, considered by some scholars to represent the army and the politics of the Pope, and links them with the miserable destiny of the mice or even worse.

The poet's harsh invectives against foreign invaders as well as those who would debase or destroy Italy from within derived from his intense love for his country and her highly civilized traditions. To Leopardi, who firmly believed that the original human state was savage and that civilization is the gradual and heroic conquest of Humanity, the naturalistic optimism of a Rousseau and the idealism of his contemporaries seemed not only absurd but dangerous. Such a doctrine could lead mankind back to barbarism, causing it to slip from a level of culture attained by so much effort.

Describing the total indifference of the dead souls before the questions of Leccafondi, Leopardi demonstrates the futility of concerning oneself with the hereafter. In this last period he thus defined to his friend Ranieri his intellectual materialism: the thinking principle is nothing else but matter, the ideas of the soul, of immortality, of an all-providing God, etc., are deliriums of the human mind, and Nature rather than friendly to man is his principal executioner. [7] Having lost his faith in God, Leopardi was left with only his faith in human potential, in a culture which has been tested by millenary experience and which must be conquered anew by the heroic effort, both individual and collective, of each succeeding generation. His contemporaries, instead, were preaching easy ways out, creating an illusory world which could only bring more disappointment and despair.

Leopardi's satiric attitude had its source in his detachment from others, in his refusal to espouse the ideals of his time and to adhere enthusiastically to what was going on around him. Anxious to discover the very meaning of human life, he perceived other men too attached to the materialistic and practical concerns of

[7] See F. Moroncini's introduction to *Opere minori, approvate di Giacomo Leopardi*, Vol. I: *Poesie* (Bologna: Cappelli, 1931), p. xlvii.

daily living. Preoccupied with the absolute and the universal, he found others too wrapped-up in their own immediate self-interest. He could only laugh at Man, who despite the discovery of Copernicus and the cruel evidence of Vesuvius, continued to view himself as the center of the universe, as a creature with special privileges enjoying a destiny superior to that of any other animal under the sun and favored by God with so many gifts on earth and even in heaven. The whole description of the underworld of the animals located on the fabulous island of Atlantis is a flavorful satire of human pride and man's radicated belief in his own immortality.

In the tradition of Aesop and Phaedrus, Leopardi portrayed human beings as animals, for example in the "Dialogo di un cavallo e di un bue" ("Dialogue between a Horse and an Ox"), in which a parallel is drawn between people and animals, which, after they have been fattened, are slaughtered. But by now it should be clear that the poet's reduction of man to animal form and proportion was not the simple adoption of a popular literary device. The form was a natural one for Leopardi, in whose opinion man behaves not too differently from the lower animals, like mice, crabs, frogs, birds, and fish, concerned with his own needs and resorting without pity to the law of the jungle. Like mice, men are ready to adjust to no matter what form of life or government in order to eat. Cheese and polenta were the true ideals of the majority of the mice, the rest was only rhetoric. And the crabs, endowed with the strength of their shells, were with great ferocity imposing their barbarism on the mice in the name of law and order. Leopardi saw the men of his century behaving no better than mice and crabs, yet preaching human progress and utopia, a new paradise on earth as well as in heaven. He felt instead that unless man becomes truly civilized through a continuous endeavor to rise above his bestial instincts, unless he is willing to accept his modest place on earth and respect the dignity of his fellow men, he will either bring about the extermination of his race, as the mice were about to exterminate the frogs, or he will act as brutally as the crabs, chopping off limbs in order to maintain the so-called balance of power.

The satiric tone of the *Paralipomeni* is accompanied and at times overwhelmed by the poet's desolation before the wretchedness of the human condition. The utter vanity of the war of the mice against the crustaceans reflects this disheartened attitude of the poet towards humanity, doomed to a blind and painful existence. In the figure of Daedalus, the only human being in the animal epic, we may perceive very clearly the anguish of mankind. Disgusted by the superficiality of his fellow men, Daedalus prefers to live alone, and he prefers the languages of the animals to human dialogue. More than representing Rousseau, as Boffito [8] has suggested, Daedalus personifies many of the ideas and feelings of Leopardi himself. In his visit to the underworld, we may well see that Daedalus, like the poet, preferred the world of the dead to the world of the living, which can have meaning only if there is mutual understanding and fraternal collaboration.

In the poetry of his youth Leopardi sang of his personal sorrow before the gradual vanishing of his "speranze" and his "ameni inganni." Now in his maturity he chants the miserable destiny of the whole of mankind blindly in search of an illusory progress. The individual sadness that permeated the lyrics of his youth has been universalized, and in the satire of the reactionary crabs and the liberal mice lives an awareness of a deeper and more virile drama, whose terms surpass the easy optimism and humanitarianism of Leopardi's contemporaries as well as of the "new believers" of any age.

---

[8] G. Boffito, "Il Dedalo moderno nei 'Paralipomeni' di Giacomo Leopardi," *Giornale storico della letteratura italiana*, CXI (1938), 76-85.

CANTO I

1   When the ranks of the vanquisher mouse had been dispersed by
the crabs, come to reintegrate the routed troops of the frogs, who
had never before met them, as he who is father to all willed, [1]
and the lovely institutions overthrown, and the lances scattered
over the battlefield with the berets and the mousy tails and the
whiskers,

2   bleeding, through every village fled the mice, galloping towards
evening, so that before vespers you might have seen the whole
shore blacken with them; as often on a wall, where the golden
sphere of the autumn sun shines most brightly, you see a dark
cloud of flies, troublesome, veil in shadow the beautiful ray of
sunlight.

3   As the papal army which the German Colli [2] led to strike the
Frenchman head-on, having moved their heels from Faenza, where
they first saw the French banners unfurled, had, after great toil,
caught its breath for the first time in Ancona, preceded there by
Colli in fervid, flying wheels, shouting, "Forward march, forward
march";

---

[1] Jove.

[2] Michele Colli (1738-1808), from Vigevano, general in the Austrian
army who commanded the Austrian and Piedmontese troops in the campaign
of 1796 against the army of Bonaparte. Here the poet refers to the
retreat of the papal trops led by General Colli from Faenza to Ancona in
February, 1797. For a colorful description of these events which Leopardi
heard from his father, Monaldo, who witnessed them firsthand, see the
latter's *Autobiografia e Dialoghetti*, a cura di A. Briganti (Bologna: Cappelli, 1972), pp. 102-115.

4   or as not too long ago the Flemish people, [3] who had sneered at
    wretched Naples, [4] at the sight of the Dutch army swiftly started
    out again on the road that they had traveled, and did not rest
    their feet before the long-invoked French aid arrived; so the mice
    from valley to valley for more than a hundred miles turned their
    backs on destiny.

5   Gone was the night, and on the second day the air was already
    beginning to darken when a soldier, called Looker-Around, found
    himself fleeing over a height. Either out of courage or because in
    the world fear is defeated by weariness, he stopped, and eager
    from habit to espy, he was the first of his race to turn his muzzle.

6   And upright on two feet, with attentive eyes, looking as far as
    he could, this way and that, in all four directions, he searched
    water and land, mountain and plain. He scrutinized the forests,
    the lakes, and the streams, the vast fields and the ocean, and he
    didn't see any foreign being except some butterflies and many
    wasps wandering below through the valley.

7   He didn't see any crabs, nor any little crabs, nor any sign of
    enemy troops in any direction. In the direction of the camp only
    the evening breeze was caressing the branches and the grass,
    whispering gently and soothing between his ears the hair of the
    brave soldier. The sky was cloudless, its western part reddish,
    and the sea calm.

8   He felt reinvigorated, and at the sight of such quiet beauty
    Looker-Around took courage again. And when, looking around
    the landscape four times with good result, he understood that
    every suspicion was inopportune and empty, he dared shout to
    his heroic companions, so much he believed his own eyes.

------

[3] Leopardi alludes to the flight of the Belgians before the Dutch army
in August, 1831. They retreated until the army of Louis-Philippe of France
arrived.

[4] The poet may be alluding to the remark of a Belgian deputy who
said that the Belgians were not Neapolitans, meaning that they would not
behave as the Neapolitans at Tolentino (May 3, 1814).

9 Not with so much joy did the ten thousand [5] who by their own strength returned to the European shores, having escaped over so vast a land the arms and snares of the Persian king, hear the voice, which from row to row became louder, of those who, first to scale the heights from which the sea was discovered, cried, as one who believes that he sees his salvation, "Sea, sea!";

10 as the mice, by then utterly exhausted from weariness and fear, heard the cry of the brave scout — to which the sea caverns resounded with the whole shore — that all around, as far as the eye could see, it was quiet and safe, that they should draw together and stop, and that from the mountain they should again show their brow.

11 Some on the knoll and some at the foot of the slope, the fugitives, to whom fear, in one day, on a deserted path, had shown a thousand shores and a thousand rivers, came together from several directions. Still disoriented, and uncertain, and weary and half-dead from the run, they started to discuss among themselves the present need and danger.

12 Already the star of Venus was appearing before the other stars and the moon. The whole shore was silent, and only the murmur of a lagoon could be heard and the shrill mosquito, coming out from the middle of the forest into the dark air. The serene image of sweet Hesperus was shining gracefully in the lake.

13 The mice were still silent, almost afraid of waking the crabs, although they were far away, and quietly they were talking mostly with their tails and their hands, marveling at that horrible army of greedy and strange beasts, and trying to find a solution to each need of their common destiny.

14 Ham-Eeater, who, I believe, was once called Ham-Eater the First, had died in battle, as you have read in the poem of Homer. I

---

[5] Allusion to the retreat of the Greeks described by Xenophon in the *Anabasis*. Having escaped from the Persians (401 B. C.), they reached Pontus Euxinus, where they embarked for Thrace.

mean the king of the mice. And when he died he had not chosen anyone to bear the burden of the kingdom, nor had he left behind an heir to whom the gods owed the royal seat.

15   Indeed there survived him a daughter, named Millstone-Licker, married to Bread-Muncher and mother of that one whose great glory still flies from mouth to mouth among men, Crumb-Stealer the Fair, whose death alone caused the war between the mice and the frogs to break out. All this likewise you either already know or you may read at leisure in Homer.

16   But a German philologist — one of those who demonstrate that the German and Greek races and languages once were brothers and even the same in the beginning, and that Rome was a German city — with many fine arguments and with a beautiful diploma proves that for a long time already the Salic law [6] had been in effect among the mice.

17   What do the systems, the conjectures, and the theories of the German people not prove? Thanks to them, we not only one day know everything about what is obscure and the next day nothing, but even in what is clear they constantly create doubts and fears and darkness: indeed in everything it is recognized very clearly that the world is fruit of German seed.

18   Therefore first of all, being in such dire straits, the miserable troops were forced for their common salvation to give all their attention to providing themselves with a new leader: harsh necessity, which for their survival condemns men and beasts to slavery and, as the price of life itself, deprives the world of the greatest good [7] for which life is alive.

19   For the time being they didn't want to elect a permanent leader, nor could they, but to wait until, having returned to Rat City, where most of them were born, they would have chased away

---

[6] A principle of traditional law, which goes back to the Salian Franks, according to which women are excluded from succession to the throne.
[7] liberty.

fear, and the frogs and the waters and along with them the barbarous and wicked crab, nor did they believe that it would be very long before they would have put the whole matter behind them.

20 Meanwhile they were content to entrust the camp, the success of their return, and the power to decide on present plans and actions to a military leader. As, when the sea darkens, a crew tossed by contrary winds follows the shrill cry of him who, giving his orders, in the peril guides the mast.

21 Chunk-Stealer [8] was chosen to command the thousands and thousands of mice: Chunk-Stealer, who, as Homer proclaims, was the Achilles of that battlefield. For a long time because of him widow frogs shed bitter tears over the entire lake, and it is said that even today among the frogs it is a terrible thing to give the name Chunk-Stealer.

22 By no means would a mother name her newborn frog Chunk-Stealer, as you hear every moment sweet voices here calling Hannibal and Arminius. [9] Thus fault or destiny has extinguished in this land for three hundred years that noble patriotic feeling which is father of every praise and which earned much glory.

23 Is there no Julius or Pompeius, no Camillus, Germanicus, or Pius, under whose name she who bore them to such nobility might have her sons' hair washed? * To see if some day the memory might instill valor in them, and if by any chance base desire and lust might be conquered by the laughter which a great name sullied with mud usually evokes?

---

[8] Under this name most scholars see Joachim Murat or Gabriele Pepe.

[9] Arminius (18 B. C.? — A. D. 19) was the chief of the ancient tribe of the Cherusci. After rendering good services to the Romans, he became one of their most dreadful enemies, inflicting on them a major defeat in the famous battle of the Teutoburg Forest (9 A. D.) where three legions, led by the Consul Quintus Varus, were completely destroyed.

* baptized.

24   Meanwhile in Lake Trasimeno a foreign traveler [10] is deliberately bathing because he remembers with pleasure our slaughter which filled that water, which, if one views the matter truthfully, still does not seem to console Zama and Carthage. [11] And that bather could also swim in the Metauro and salute Spoleto along the way.

25   If it pleased us to follow for fun this method by which others find solace, we could go sporting in many waters and warm ourselves by the fires of many forests, and we could, traveling, refresh ourselves a bit in many fields from east to west and along the way remember more than one triumph achieved in our land and in theirs.

26   So much hatred of the Italian name inflames the breasts of foreigners that they rejoice over that loss of which they have no share of glory, just because it was ours. Many nations went through difficult times and became depraved through long suffering, but not one could be shown to be the object of as much hatred as ours.

27   And this occurs because, although subjugated, enslaved, and lacerated she sits in misfortune, still whatever of mortal nature is greatest must be called Italian; still the glory of eternal Rome so shines that it eclipses all others, and Europe, unduly proud with us, in every region preserves the stamp of Italy.

28   Not only Rome but unarmed Italy, with her enlightenment and her learning, defeated barbarism, and in splendid dress [12] returned once again queen; and she laughed a long time at the clumsy foreigner, who now dares to disparage her in her misfortune, and

---

[10] At least one critic, Ettore Allodoli, has suggested that Leopardi was thinking about Byron. At Lake Trasimeno the Romans were defeated by Hannibal in 217 B. C. during the Second Punic War.

[11] Leopardi says that this traveler might think of Rome's victories as well as of her defeats. The Romans defeated the Carthaginians at Zama in 202 B. C. Hasdrubal was conquered and killed on the Metaurus and Hannibal was turned back at Spoleto.

[12] The Renaissance.

saw that to her own children residence in other countries seemed like unhappy exile.

29 Foreigners feel their every memory to be a trifle in comparison with those to which Italy is heir, their every country to be a child with respect to her who exceeds every greatness; and well they see that if as many talents as heaven bestows were not strangled in the cradle, if Italy were for just awhile set free, she would return queen the third time. [13]

30 Thence the implacable hatred, thence the anger and the ironic laughter with which others offend her who, shackled, on the sand, with tongue or hand no longer defends herself. [14] And those who show greater pity for her than they feel and kindle hope in the ignorant among us, would rather see the Judean people flourish again than aid Italian honor.

31 There beneath the imposing structures of Rome, Pigmy, [15] lifting his thoughtless forehead, swinging his body, strikes with his little rod monuments unique in the world; he seems to console himself with his words, chasing away the memory of his servitude. And it is natural for the immortal hostility of others to follow such greatness.

32 But Chunk-Stealer, since he had been charged with the care of his fellow companions, had the camp fortified so that the night would be secure against unexpected attacks and acts of terrorism, and then had the trembling and languishing bodies nourished with food. The latter task was an easy one, because everything is good for feeding mice.

33 Afterwards, he thought it necessary to send a messenger immediately to the hated army, in order to ask why, unprovoked, they had sided against them in the fight, whether on their own or

---

[13] She was queen of civilization in Roman times and during the Renaissance.

[14] This image is also found in "All'Italia," written by Leopardi in 1818.

[15] Leopardi makes a caricature of the presumptuous foreigners in the preceding verses.

in alliance with the frogs, whether by mistake or deliberately, whether they intended to advance further or to return to their own land, whether they wanted peace or war from the mice.

34   Count Bottom-Licker, Lord of Smoke-Weigher and Wind-Sifter, [16] was in the camp. He was a rare mouse in his day, a marvel of profound thought and doctrine. He knew the laws and conditions of both hemispheres, and he read more than two hundred newspapers, for the study of which he had opened in his country what we call nowadays a reading room. [17]

35   A public reading room, with the regulation that, except for newspapers, no book containing more than two pages be received within its walls, because he believed that a writer attuned to the universal political, economic, and moral needs could not go beyond such a limit.

36   However, little by little, partly induced by friends and partly by his own considerateness, he allowed the historical novel to lodge with the newspapers. It could run up to eight or ten volumes. Finally, as demonstrated by that learned writer whom I call to witness above, he made room for German poetry.

37   A poetry which in age somewhat exceeds the various Semitic and Sanskritic poetries. It alone appeared to the count to have for its own glory the revival of good taste in opposition to the fallacious Horatian song, by deliberately giving, merely for the sake of novelty, tunas to farms and rams to the sea; [18] great labor, and from minds rare on earth.

38   He was also a fanatic admirer of the German arts and, spending lavishly, surrounded himself with them, because, according to

---

[16] The typical figure of the liberal and progressive thinker of Leopardi's time. Some critics have recognized in this character Marquis Gino Capponi, whom Leopardi satirized in the "Palinody."

[17] Probable allusion to the Gabinetto Vieusseux in Florence, with which Leopardi was familiar.

[18] A free translation of the passage in Horace's *Ars poetica*, 30: "delphinum silvis appingit, fluctibus aprum."

the above-mentioned author, the obelisks were not yet standing nor had the pyramids yet lifted their heads when the arts already had their seat in Germany, where we see that the sense of beauty is finer than it was among the Greeks or the Latins.

39 His library was furnished with books of very beautiful appearance, bound in various styles, and so exquisite, with gilt, ribbons, and every other embellishment, that even if the contents were quadrupled it would not be enough to match the value of the cover. And this was rightly so, because not in the pages but in that part was its usefulness.

40 Not to mention the museum, the archives, the menagerie of wild animals, the botanic gardens, and the portico, where you could see with his enormous mustache and giant tail, the colossal statue of Lampstand, ancient little philosopher mouse, and of the same a fresco painting, also by a German chisel and brush.

41 The count was very much absorbed in thought about his species, he was a moral philosopher and a philomouse; he praised nature for demonstrating here on earth her celebrated power in creating the mouse, whose works, talent, and glorious condition he admired; and he predicted that after not too long a time the great destiny which nature reserved to the mouse would be fulfilled.

42 But he had ever at heart the continuous progress of the mouse mind, which he was satisfied to expect chiefly from the swift pens of the journalists; and he always affirmed that hypotheses, systems, and feeling are beneficial to such progress, and that analyses, reason, and experience stifle knowledge and make it cloudy.

43 A good mouse, on the other hand, and far removed from any philosophical hypocrisy, and frank on the whole and sincere, although a courtisan and brought up in the midst of intrigues; attached to the common people, and always approachable by anyone; and, if we may be allowed to say so, human; caring little about money and much about honor, generous, and patriotic.

44 He had gone as ambassador of his own king to the king of the frogs before the military rage had severed the friendly ties between

the two kingdoms; and having returned to his master, as soon as the war broke out, he dwelt among the soldiers and beneath the tents, until the entire army found safety in swift flight.

45   At present, to his companions, searching for someone to whom they might assign in the name of all the task of going as their speaker to the general of the crab camp and of trying to ward off any new harm for the rest of them, no one for his wisdom and virtue appeared more suitable for that than the count, who was held in the highest esteem by all.

46   Thus, raising one of the front feet as a sign of approval, according to the ancient custom, those troops unanimously elected him messenger of the army to the enemy. And he did not turn down the assignment, although he was going to expose himself to great risk: going into a hostile camp, unprotected, among people ignorant of every custom and right of other nations.

47   And although physically exhausted and very much in need of rest, he nevertheless did not want to defer the departure. After a very short nap on the soft grass, he got up in the middle of the night and, with only a few of his servants, leaving behind the hill all silent and sleeping, he descended, and started the journey through the solitary country.

CANTO II

1 More than half of the nocturnal hours had passed, and the stars, chaste and silent, were bending their course towards the ocean, shining over the deserted plain. Deserted to the mouse indeed, but nearby and afar in the woods, in the bushes and young trees, the cares of the day were lulling many wild animals of the land and many birds.

2 Here and there in the distant fields, on the road, and over the hills, more than one farmhouse could be discerned whitening amid the green in the dark air. And from time to time from each one could be heard through the silence a barking of dogs and searching in the gardens, and in the stables chains clanking and mares stomping.

3 The count was trotting on his perilous journey, hurrying his four soles with his servants. On foot I mean, because riding on horseback is the privilege of man, who among as many beasts as the earth, the air, and the sea produce, alone by his very nature is a horseman, as, it reasonably follows, he alone by nature is a carriage rider.

4 It was May, which infuses love with life, and far away could be heard singing the cuckoo, mysterious bird, which in the deep of the forest sighs with an almost human sound and, like some nocturnal spirit, wanders around and confuses the shepherd, who in vain pants to chase after him, and his singing does not last, for it is born in the springtime and summer finds it come to an end.

5 As to Ulysses and the cruel Diomedes,[1] when they were going through the treacherous shades of night to the new trojan camp, seeking danger and unusual events, the bird which shakes itself and screeches seemed, croaking, to bring a sign of good luck from Minerva, to whom both had appealed with prayers for help;

6 so the mouse, who was accustomed to observing voices and signs with great attention — I don't really know from which god or which goddess, mouse or she-mouse or of like nature — firmly hoped, and he needed such hope to lift his heart from fear, that the cuckoo, which the mice hold divine, would come as messenger of a not evil destiny.

7 But already behind thickets and hillocks, ancient and weary the moon was climbing in the sky and over the grassy ridges and small branches was spreading an uneven and languishing light, giving them shadows neither clear nor very distinct one from the other. Nonetheless it outshone all the stars and longed for came to the traveler.

8 However, since light is not very welcome to mice, the count, who trotting on foot, as I have said, was retracing through valley and over mountain the tracks which a short while before, forced to flee, he had left with much swifter paws, did not rejoice very much over it, and the place reminded him now of many losses, now of many fears on that flight.

9 But above all he was moved by pity and by sadness, seeing at each step, on the road or not far from it, a little mouse either dead or dying, one by wounds, another by fatigue led to his mortal destiny, to whom the moon with its languid and half-lit splendor seemed to be paying its final respects.

---

[1] Leopardi refers to the episode of Book X of the *Iliad* which narrates that when Ulysses and Diomedes went secretly during the night to explore the Trojan camp, they were reassured by the voice of a heron, considered by them a good omen from Minerva.

10   Thus, silent, turning over in his head profound philosophical thoughts and calling for and hoping from the journalists of both hemispheres an efficient, complete, and quick remedy for the deadly discord of the races and empires, he traveled for so long that night, little by little yielding, gave way to morning.

11   The roosters were all awake singing through the countryside and the little birds were starting all over again together the customary dances over the meadows to the murmur of the breeze, the purple, fresh dawn was making ready for the day the sempiternal paths and it could not be long before the king of the years [2] would raise high his forehead,

12   when the mouse, gazing from a knoll not very far ahead down on the plain, saw that which, although he was searching for it, he would have preferred not yet to have seen, which now seemed to banish everything from his heart except fear, not only because of what it was but partly and mostly because it was present before he expected it.

13   He saw the camp of the crabs, who, as soon as they had put to flight the once vanquishing troops of the mice, towards Rat City, where it seemed to them that the fugitives had headed, decided to lead their arms and banners, advancing behind by forced marches, and following them, they were less than one night away from the place where the run had brought them.

14   The count was shaking and already the servants had turned their backs on the terrible sight. Neither wall, nor rampart, nor trench could have held back that lazy and wretched folk, but the count, always obedient to his own honor, as valor is acquired through shame, having first taken heart himself, threw himself on his servants shouting, and forced them to turn back.

15   And having seen not too far away a verdant olive grove, they quickly entered it, and each one having taken with his hand or with his mouth a twig of the evergreen and descended with it

---

[2] The sun.

onto the plain, feeling a shiver go through every hair and gnashing for fear their teeth, they came to the enemy quarters.

16 The crabs had hardly noticed them when they were upon them, and without considering the right or the wrong of it, they wanted at any cost to swallow them alive along with their olive branches, or at least they would have killed them right away, if speech, which with eternal power rules the world according to its pleasure, had not come to the defense of the unfortunate captives.

17 For although the language of the crabs was barbarian and prim- itive, it was not unknown to the count, who besides being well- traveled, having been educated for the diplomatic service, as we say nowadays, had learned through study and practice every language, and even the dialects of every one of them, so that in languages he was a Mezzofanti. [3]

18 Therefore with mellifluous words and reasons he began to soften those iron hearts, which had never learned such sweet words from companions or from masters, nor knew that other people could speak the sounds of their own mother tongue and thus thought that a little crab of their own country went under the disguise of a mouse.

19 Because of this and because they saw that Bottom-Licker had glasses rooted on his nose, arms which neither men nor animals were ever in the habit of carrying to war, being from the begin- ning the characteristic emblem and honor of men of letters and therefore to mortals a sure pledge of peace and security more than the rainbow [4] or the olive or any other symbol,

20 they decided that for the moment they should refrain from shedding the blood of those foreigners. And having tied them up

---

[3] Giuseppe Gaspare Mezzofanti (Bologna, 1774-1849), well known from his early years in the seminary for his vast knowledge of and versatility in languages, taught Arab, Greek, and several Oriental languages in the Uni- versity of Bologna. In 1833 he succeeded Angelo Mai as director of the Vatican Library, and in 1838 he was made a cardinal.

[4] The rainbow and the olive were the traditional symbols of peace. Iris, in Greek mythology, was the goddess who personified the rainbow.

as shepherds or quacks never did dogs or any ferocious or rare
animal, crookedly, according to their custom, they dragged them
before the general of those marmorean lansquenets, people hostile
to walking forward. [5]

21 Strong-Claw [6] was the name of that crab, rude and at the same
time servile in appearance. Seen by him and asked who he was,
where he came from, and for what purpose, the count answered
that he came as the ambassador of his camp, and he was well
tied [7] and tighter than was necessary. However, the noble epopee
does not endure jokes.

22 He continued, saying that if someone untied him, he would show
the mandate and the letters patent. For this purpose the general
did not allow the sergeants to start disentangling him, and because
it had never happened to him to read, written documents were
not pertinent to him, but he asked by whom they had been
given and in whose name he had assumed the ambassadorial
charge.

23 He [8] said that the kingdom of the mice, their king having died
in the war and there not remaining anyone worthy to succeed him,
had deliberated on the matter in a democratic fashion and that
Chunk-Stealer, whom the entire army by vote had selected as
their leader along with himself as messenger, had certified the
mandate.

24 Hearing words such as people, votes, and elections, the chaste
lansquenet froze beneath his shell, just like a young maiden whose
tender ears a lewd enemy soldier or coachman offends with loath-

---

[5] Here Leopardi refers to the Austrians' reactionary and conservative
policies.

[6] Strong-Claw is commonly identified with General Bianchi, who defeated the army of Murat at Tolentino.

[7] Leopardi makes a pun, which cannot be translated into English, on
the word *legato*, which means *legate* or *ambassador* and is the past
participle of *legare*, which means to *tie (up)*.

[8] The count.

some and awful tongue, spreading all around mud and foul odors. She blushes, turns pale, and shrinks within herself.

25   And he said to the count, "However I look at it, I do not find here any legitimate power. Not to mention the rest of it, I do not approve receiving as ambassador one who has been elected by many." Then, as if he were chasing from his sight a shameful thing or a dreadful and strange monster, he had the mice removed and shut up underground in chains and watched very closely.

26   Having done this, he notified his king by the shortest way of the unexpected event and begged him to order what he would have done. That king was, as far as I can determine in my research, one of the third dynasty called Without-Heads and was the nineteenth of that name to sit on the throne. [9]

27   The king answered that, since the seat was vacant, the one elected by the camp should be received as ambassador; that soon the kingdom, either voluntarily or under force, would elect another master; that he should never conclude any treaty with them before that happened; that on every other point he should do what was commanded him before.

28   This order reached the general in the place where the count had found him, because in that very place he remained awaiting what would be ordered by the fount of power, [10] according to whose will, as soon as he received word, the deeds followed in agreement and quickly. He removed the prisoners from underground, untied them, and received the count, untied, in his presence.

29   Who on request explained to the general the motives and the purpose of his coming, asking what destiny, what force or what violation of territory or boundary, what damage to property or

---

[9] This is a direct reference to the then Emperor of Austria, Francis I of Lorraine, who belonged to the third dynasty of the Hapsburgs and was the nineteenth emperor of that family.

[10] By the emperor.

bodily harm, what pact or alliance, or finally what mistake had brought upon the heads of the unwary and tired mice the rage of the crabs.

30 The general of the encrusted people spit, looked around, and composed himself; and with mountainous gravity he answered in this manner, or almost like it: "Mister Mouse, we know nothing of all that you ask, but by giving aid to the frogs the crabs have fought to maintain the balance of power."

31 "What does this mean?" continued the count. "Did you think that if the race of the frogs were destroyed by us, perhaps the waters of the lake or of the marsh or of the canal or of the river or of the fountain would change state and inundate the plain, or dry up, or return to the mountain, or undergo some other change more harmful and strange?"

32 "Not balance of water but of land," answered the crab, "is the motive of fighting and the law of peace and of war, which I shall explain with a comparison. You must imagine that the whole world with all that it contains resembles a large scale, not with one pan or two, but with a flock of them, corresponding to each other, some larger and some smaller.

33 Each pan receives an animal, which is to say a power of the earth. In one a mouse, in another an owl, and in some other a frog is placed, inside here a crab and there a wagtail, one animal balanced with the other in such a way that with different weights all of the countries together are in balance.

34 Now when one animal becomes fatter than he used to be, with another's property or with his own, and another either accidentally or struck by the first becomes so skinny that he rises up, it is necessary to jump immediately on the first one, I mean on the one who is overloading his side, and by cutting off his feet, his tail, or his wings, make the scales level off again.

35 These amputated limbs are carried to the one who, becoming thin, was underweight, or are eaten by a stronger animal who is

not yet a good counterbalance to another or who, after eating
them, becomes big enough to stretch out on two pans at the same
time and keep safe the balance on this side with his buttocks and
on the other with his belly."

36 "Supposing all this were true," answered Count Bottom-Licker
to the crab, "what divinity ordained that the nation of the crabs
preside over the general balance of the worlds and that they
devote themselves to observing if the mice or the frogs are larger
or rounder than they should be, in order to extract from them
the flesh or the nose or the eyes?"

37 "We," answered the general, "are precisely the policemen and
the executioners of Europe, and we practice this art." Note, wise
reader, that I do not know at all if he said of Europe or of
another place, because, to tell the truth, I have never succeeded,
for all the old maps I have turned through, in finding the region
and the climate where the events which I am putting into rhyme
took place.

38 But I have said of Europe following the common usage of our language. Now, to return to the language of the crab: "In our
custody," he added "is the constancy of the animals in their
original state, and when something unusual or some discrepancy
is noticed, wherever it may be, there the armed crab runs and
restores things to their original order."

39 "Who charged you with this?" asked the count. "The shell," he
said, "with which we are dressed, and the fact of being without
brain or forehead, secure, invariable, as petrified as coral and
mountain crystal, famous on all shores for our hardness: this
makes us pillars and foundations of the stability of other peoples."

40 "Now let's put aside reasons and words," went on the other, "and
let's get down to the facts. What does the king of the crabs want
today from the mice? Does he still want war and slaughter at
any price? Or does he consent, as others are wont to do, to

discuss here accord and friendship? And in such a case, what condition of accord and friendship does he propose to us?"

41 The general of the crabs spit again, adjusted himself, and spoke in this manner: Soon a new master must be elected by your race. It is forever forbidden to him to wage wars or quarrels with the frogs. Their future will be decided by our master, whom it pleased to receive in his guardianship their lands and waters.

42 You will lodge in Rat City a garrison of three thousand crabs and you will place in their care the castle and any other fortified buildings, if you have them, within the walls. They shall have from you food and drink according to their thirst, with whatever else is required by their nature, and double pay for each day as long as they stay among you."

43 Having heard the count say that he did not have the authority from his people to agree to so much and that it was necessary to sign a truce in order that he might in the meantime inform the others, the general answered that he granted fifteen days' time during which he would not move his army, but if the period passed without results, he would advance on Rat City by force of arms.

44 Thus ended the conversation between Bottom-Licker and the warrior Strong-Claw. Without delay the messenger of the mice turned his thoughts towards his return, having set his mind entirely on the utilization of the truce. He quickly assembled his servants. On leaving he saw a few frogs who had come into the camp for business.

45 He recognized them because he had become acquainted with them when he went among them as ambassador, and now he heard from them of the particular care and the great favor given the frogs at their own expense by the king of the crabs, who under the pretext of protecting the allied state from the mice, had put everything under his control.

46 And that he could never get enough gold and did not pay any attention to their king. The count felt pity for them and with sincere words heartily thanked the gods of his country, who had sent over the mice a calamity less cruel than the protection given to others. Bid farewell by the frogs, he then took to the open road and left the camp behind.

CANTO III

1 Meanwhile Chunk-Stealer had led his troops back into Rat City to safety, where for more than a day and a night great sorrow was mixed with great happiness. Some rejoice at seeing their loved ones again, some with unrestrained tears call their dead brothers, others their fathers or husbands, others their children, and others grieve for the kingdom and its honor.

2 Rat City [1] — to describe for you the lay and the site of the land — was with admirable structure all walled up inside a live rock, which by art or by nature was hollowed out so that it contained, as if hidden within the womb, a large cave forever concealed from the sun and from the stars.

3 Try to remember, if you ever crossed the mountain which still keeps the name of Hasdrubal, there where Livius and Nero scattered over the countryside the arms and the hopes of the African, [2] by the road, subterranean and resonant, where the heavenly light does not accompany the traveler, where with great skill the mountain is open from one side to the other;

4 or if nearby Naples, there where a loving faith places the tomb of Virgil, you ever saw the passage which often resounds with the thunder that strikes all around from Vesuvius, where, at his entrance, night suddenly falls down on the head of the trav-

---

[1] Rat City is a satiric representation of the city of Naples.
[2] Hasdrubal, brother of Hannibal, was defeated and killed in battle on the Metaurus in 207 B. C. during the Second Punic War. Livius Salinator and G. Claudius Nero were the consuls who defeated him.

eler, who sees, as if a faraway speck of a feeble light, the other opening through which later on he comes out into the open again;

5   and you will have images enough of the place where Rat City was founded. Its entrance was through four openings on four sides of the mountain, which were so skillfully stopped up that it remained not only closed but concealed to everyone, so that the only thing that betrayed the city on the outside was the odor.

6   Within stood royal palaces and buildings of very fine architecture, innumerable colleges and hospitals, always empty but immense in size, statues, triumphal columns and arches, and monuments of every sort. Upon a round rock was the castle, marvelously fortified by its site, and beautiful.

7   As he who, having crossed the ridge of the Apennines near Foligno, takes the delightful open road through the cultivated valley whose course is broken by the hill of Spoleto, [3] if he lifts his happy gaze, guided upwards to the left, to the steep shoulders of a rock, white, bare of any flowers, of any grass, sees something that he will always remember:

8   the city of Trevi, [4] which with a scene of lofty roofs occupies the windy summit in such a way that all around with the extreme back of the farthest buildings she lowers her feet to the ground, yet sits in view clear and serene and seems almost an enchantment to the traveler. Churches and palaces shine in the bright daylight, and windows sparkle all around.

9   Such, but deprived of daylight, you would have seen to be the castle of which I speak, solidly built upon the summit of the polished rock, showing more than is customary around the edge so that it seemed to drop down with it. Only from one side, by

---

[3] Foligno and Spoleto are towns in the province of Perugia. The valley of the Maroggia is broken by the hill on which Spoleto is located.

[4] Trevi is a small town on the eastern slope of the valley of the Clitumnus in the province of Perugia.

a narrow path, with fear and sweat, could anyone climb up there.

10 Each one of us sees in his own room that the mice don't have much need of light, because they are accustomed to doing all their business while closed up in the wardrobes and the pantries, and when the oil-lamps and the candles have been put out, they come out at night to do their dance. Yet if light was needed there now and then, everyone provided himself with torches.

11 Thus beneath Resina, which covers the very noble ruins of Herculaneum with humble houses and taverns, pilgrims descend by the flickering of dim lamps to see the afflicted and yet eternally famous limbs; mansions and theaters and temples and colonnades still denied to the brightness of day. [5]

12 Surely if Germanic or British soil covered these ruins of ours, man would no longer have to use torches in order to visit the ancient damage, and whatever the expense and trouble, Pompei, whom fate inscribed to the same destiny, would have returned to the sunlight in entirety and not just a small part of her.

13 I shall not declaim the everlasting shame and disgrace of Italy, but of those who value dishonest treasure more than bringing to light the mystery of golden antiquity and, once unearthed, showing again to the foreigner the Italian greatness. May heaven grant them their just deserts, if indeed that is not vainly implored of heaven.

14 And may the hypocritical scoundrels be rewarded not with laughter and with anger, of which they always had plenty, but with other injuries, since on their account all of Europe for so many, many years has been sighing in vain for the papyri, over which cautiously they rave on the mercenary seats, chasing away

---

[5] The village of Resina was built on the ruins of Herculaneum. The limbs, or ruins, are afflicted because they have been despoiled of their many art treasures.

everyone else; breed on account of which I would even be sorry if hangmen and gallows should fail us. [6]

15   Returning to the mice, to whom it is easy to return from the shelves of these cunning fellows, [7] Rat City dominated in that time the principal cities from north to south, or had very few of them as equals. It was the proper and natural abode of the mice, where for the most part the kingdom and the flower of the mouse people resided.

16   Because far from there few or none of their lineage had permanent residence, except in colonies, where in that time people used to terminate some trip or other. You know well that for a long time a number of civilized and wise nations had one circuit of walls enclosing an entire kingdom, which extended the empire through colonies.

17   You can imagine what an immense crowd Rat City lodged within her walls. Unfortunately the word *statistics* had not yet been heard in those days, [8] but it is considered a sure thing that the number was several million, and today Rat City is named along with Nineveh, Babylon, Memphis, and Rome.

18   Therefore, the army of the mice having returned, as I have said, to the city and the beating of hands and chests in the cafés, in the houses, and in the streets having ceased, every other feeling yielding to patriotism, or to fear, as more often happens, every thought and word were turned to looking for the return of the messenger.

19   Because it seemed that everything consisted in knowing the enemy's intention and that without such knowledge every counsel

---

[6] Here the author attacks the members of the Academy of Herculaneum, who would not publish the papers that all European scholars were anxiously awaiting.

[7] Because, like these narrow-minded yet shrewd academicians, mice often inhabit the dusty shelves of deserted libraries.

[8] For the author's satire on statistics, see the "Palinody to Marquis Gino Capponi" vv. 138-145, and the "Dialogue between Tristan and a Friend."

was random and useless, nor did it seem that discussing a durable
government of the kingdom could have any meaning if the storm
which seemed to threaten on all sides did not first quiet down.

20   But since in those days they vainly longed for the count's return
to his homeland, while he, having fallen into the hands of wild
people, as a prisoner underground was awaiting orders from the
king, and since anxiety and fear of the unknown and of the far
away were increasing and it even appeared necessary to organize
the state to endure war, in case there should be war as well;

21   Chunk-Stealer along with the leaders of the city decided not to
delay any longer, nor to invite new troubles, but to assemble the
people at once and to explain in public the grave and capital
matters of the government, so that in the event the army should
return to the dangers outside, things would already be settled
inside.

22   Chunk-Stealer, because of his many noble and powerful relatives,
and because he had enjoyed the favor of the soldiers for a long
time, and because of that arm which had removed from the world
so many enemies, would indeed have been able to hold on to
that already sovereign power that fate had placed in his hands.

23   And not a few generals, princes, and barons, coming to him
spontaneously, encouraged him and declared themselves ready
to support his reasons. But with marvelous valor the hero rejected
the vile persuasions of others and left entirely to the common
will the formation of the state and the appropriate command.

24   Worthy therefore of eternal praise was he, to whom ancient and
modern history has no one equal or even to compare, as far as I
can now recall, apart from three of illustrious and immortal fame,
Timoleon the Corinthian [9] and Andrea Doria [10] on this side of
the ocean, and Washington [11] on the American side.

---

[9] Timoleon (400-337 B. C.), Corinthian general, freed Syracuse from
the tyrant Dionysius II, and when asked by the Syracusans to rule the city,
would not accept their offer.
[10] Andrea Doria, having liberated Genoa (1528) with the aid of Charles V

25 For modesty, for true splendor of deeds and probity of mind, I won't deny or fail to say that, although Italian, Doria is the least worthy among them. But perfect goodness was not allowed by that wretched century, when cruelty reigned with mysterious intrigue, and cowardice of thought with boldness.

26 Its history is a desert revealing no act of uncorrupted virtue, reason for which above any other everyone likes to recall events and deeds. Boredom and oblivion in the end cover the rest, except for this unique splendor of heroic deds, with whose holy light the desert of which I speak is not blessed on any side.

27 It is a wonder that Morris of Saxony, [12] who with a thousand shameful acts and betrayals acquires a large part of liberty for his people, comes into your view there, Egmont [13] and Orange, [14] intent on their own greatness, liberating their oppressed and miserable country, and that better one [15] who with a strong arm sends the first Duke of Florence to his death.

28 Nor is any cause for admiration to be found if he does not seem to you worthy of admiration who, inheriting, renews the grandeur of antiquity and not the virtues, and who, showing himself in-

---

from the French domination, would not become ruler of the city, asking instead to be only one of the five censors.

[11] George Washington refused the royal crown offered to him by the Constituent Assembly, in favor of a federal constitution.

[12] Morris of Saxony (1521-1553) led a revolt of princes against Charles V and defeated the Emperor in the Tyrol. Afterwards, he faced the powerful Albert of Brandenburg and died of wounds two days after the battle at Sievershausen.

[13] Lamoral, Count of Egmont (1522-1568) served under Charles V, was ambassador to England and governor of Flanders, where he tried to reconcile Catholics and Protestants. He commanded the cavalry of the battle of St. Quentin. He was beheaded by order of the Duke of Alba.

[14] William of Orange (1533-1584), called the "Taciturn," considered by the Dutch as the father of their country and the free state. He was assassinated by a fanatic Catholic.

[15] Alessandro de' Medici (1510-1537), nephew of Pope Clement VII, was, after the capitulation of the Republic of Florence, made the first Duke of Florence by the favor of the Pope and of the Emperor Charles V. He was killed by his cousin, Lorenzino de' Medici.

ferior to the task of such a kingdom in every test — it seems that he does not know how to aim at any target — alternately conquers and loses cities, and wastes the flower of Europe in Africa. [16]

29 Not of noble heart and not of base, neither faithless nor pious, cruel nor gentle, loving neither the iniquitous nor the upright, sometimes keeping his promises, sometimes breaking them, never fond of the great nor of the fine, of deeds neither easy nor daring, he knows not how to free two princes [17] imprisoned in his power nor how to detain them.

30 At last of so much fame and power no result is seen. On the contrary, he himself throws away and of his own will gives up the great burden which exceeds his strength, and its vast domain, which vainly surpassed the ordinary, he divides and loses among more than one heir; then wrapped in monastic clothes he enjoys being buried before he is dead. [18]

31 Oh constancy, oh valor of ancient times! You knew how to make great things out of nothing. How to make nothing out of great things an age of fools learned from that day when Constantine, on a level with the most infamous examples, donated our army with our scepter to another part. [19] The effects of the true Roman Empire and of the German differ in this way.

---

[16] Charles V (1500-1558), Holy Roman Emperor (1519-1556) and King of Spain as Charles I (1516-1556). Leopardi alludes to the disastrous expedition to Algeria, in 1541.

[17] This seems to be an allusion to Francis I, imprisoned after the battle of Pavia (1527), and to Clement VII, held after the sack of Rome (1527). In the opinion of Allodoli, the poet refers to the two sons of Francis I, kept as hostages following the Treaty of Madrid (1526).

[18] In 1556, abdicating his throne, Charles V subdivided his vast empire into two parts, giving Spain and the connected states to his son, Philip II, and the other part, mainly the territory under the Austrian crown, to his brother, Ferdinand I. He then retired to a monastary in Spain, where he died after two years.

[19] Constantine transferred the seat of the Roman Empire, and consequently its military power, to Byzantium, which became Constantinople. Leopardi contrasts the ancient Roman Empire with the Holy Roman Empire.

32   Among us the great men of that dark century vie not for honor but for hatred and contempt. Nor would it be easy to judge who was responsible for the reign of hatred, if you, marvel of pride and token of heaven's anger, did not surpass everyone, oh second Philip, [20] Austrian plant, of whom Master Satan still boasts.

33   Among your contemporaries and your posterity, no one else, alive or dead, in recent times or remote, ever carried as much hatred as is gathered on your head. At the mention of your name you exacerbate every kindly face and jolt every peaceful heart, so wonderful you are at pursuing the liveliest and innermost fountain of human anger.

34   After you I crown that very great Duke of Alba [21] who, almost as if he were your rival, dares to contend with you, and proclaims to the Batavians, [22] excluding every one of them, a general pardon. Noble and salutary example, so much to the liking of the throne of your successors, which caused the new indignation and the great valor of Holland and your broken yoke.

35   But I have gotten too far away from Rat City, and so in a hurry I return there. Gathered in the market place waiting for me, oh readers, is a vast throng, which listens to or thinks it is listening to an endless chatter about government, and praises or rejects,

---

[20] Philip II (1527-1598), son of Emperor Charles V and of Isabella of Portugal, the most powerful monarch of his time, waged a war of religious oppression against the Netherlands, and beat back the Mohammedan invasion by defeating the Turks at Lepanto (1571). His attack on England failed with the defat of the Invincible Spanirh Armada in 1588.

[21] Ferdinando Alvarez de Toledo (1507-1582), Duke of Alba, valiant and very ambitious general and politician, was conisdered one of Charles V's best generals. Under Philip II he became a very influential counselor. He was governor of Milan in 1555 and led the army against Pope Paul IV and the Duke of Guise in southern Italy. Sent into the Low Countries in 1567, since they were revolting against the Spanish regime, he made himself notorious for his cruel and ferocious repression, causing the general rebellion of the population.

[22] Batavians: the Dutch. The Batavians were a Germanic people who inhabited present day Holland before Caesar. From 1795 to 1806 the Low Countries were called Batavia.

and takes counsel or believes it is taking counsel, and makes laws or firmly believes it is making them.

36 Who could describe the negotiations, the deals, the disagreements, the noise, the factions which usually occur when the herd proceeds with such elections, in order to fill whatever kind of seats, not to speak of refurnishing vacant thrones? All of this was going on among them, and I willingly pass over it.

37 Touching only on the conclusion, I'll say that after an eternal dispute from dawn to vespers, with debate now on foreign affairs, now on internal, the people decided to be governed by a new monarchy: one of those which are in part tempered by statutes called charters.

38 Whether it resembled more the statute, or constitution, [23] as we say nowadays, of England, or approximated that of France or of some other nation, with parliaments or high or low assemblies, with public election or royal appointment, double or simple, finally, as in Spain, the statute or magna carta of the mice,

39 from all that I have read concerning it among the ancients, could not be put together. This alone can be affirmed without suspicion of ignorance or of lies, that the prince was then elected by the mice, and that the new sovereignty was that which, if it were not unsuitable in verse, I would have called constitutional.

40 Bread-Muncher, [24] son-in-law of the late King Ham-Eater, was delegated to reign. As when Priam and the abundant fruit of his stem were wanting to the Trojan people, fleeing to foreign lands they all came together under the son-in-law Aeneas: because in

---

[23] Except in this octave and in the following, where the meaning requires that we adhere closely to the poet's diction, we have translated *statuto* as *constitution*, since, as Leopardi himself admits in stanza 38, *constitution* is the word in current usage.

[24] Bread-Muncher is commonly identified with Ferdinando IV of Bourbon (1751-1825), King of Naples, who after the Restoration (1816) changed his name to Ferdinando I, King of the Two Sicilies.

the end we like to believe that only the royal family is capable of ruling.

41   And once that is extinct, we look for the next of kin and then one by one the other relatives by degrees until the royal humor languishes in the most distantly related. Nor does this occur only in peace time, but when the kingdom is left bloodless through harsh treatment, then by a rough and bloody path, armed, it resorts to a new dynasty.

42   And when changing government for any other reason, it does away with the previous one, it always gathers hopeful in the shade of some plant of royal seed. Like a child who, left without the skirt which supports him and covers him, after wavering a brief time, soon crying climbs back over it with his hands and feet. [25]

43   Or as a bold and fervid mare, having gotten out of the coachman's hand for fun, returns by great leaps to her stable, where whip, and perhaps stick, welcome her, or as a bird suddenly lowers his flight from the heights denied him and voluntarily returns to the trusty cage where he has lived since his tender age.

44   I find that this one was, nevertheless, considered in ancient times to be a kind, loving, and good king, always mindful of when at the foot of the throne he had lived as a subject among subjects: grateful to all the people, thanks to whom, and not to heaven, he had come to the throne; and not unaware of others' misfortunes, nor stingy with aid.

45   And I find that against the armed enemy he defended with sincere purpose the constitution, or pact which he had accepted under oath from the citizens. Nor did he have the desire, although he had the opportunity, to rid himself of it. I say this since it exceeds others' belief and not my own.

---

[25] That is, like a child who needs the security of his mother's presence (the skirt).

CANTO IV

1 Perhaps, honorable readers, this story has caused you to wonder now and then. And as it is the habit and nature of men to pass judgment very easily, perhaps, though well-disposed towards me and friendly, you have thought more than once that I must be either a liar or a fool,

2 because I have represented the things of the mouse kingdom, which owing to their antiquity are so remote from us that, as appears clear from several indications, they may be compared with those of ancient India — the customs, the speech, the institutions, the genius, the least and the most important affairs — like ours, as if they had been yesterday or the day before yesterday.

3 But with the wonder every suspicion like a mist will be removed from your mind by reading, if you have not yet read, what the sages have recently discovered, speculating with the mere intellect on the condition of mankind: that the present civilized state of Europe must still be called primitive. [1]

4 And that those whom the common people call savages, who in the hottest and coldest lands, naked in the sun, in the wind, in the storm, and provided only with a natural roof, are happy, as soon as they are weaned from the breast, to be nourished with grass

---

[1] Here and in the following stanzas Leopardi satirizes the so called theological school of historiography, whose main exponents were De Bonald, Lamennais, and De Maistre, and according to which man, created perfect by God, fell from that paradisiac state on account of progress and civilization and only through religion might regain his original happy condition.

and worms, and fear the breezes and the branches and that, melted by the sun, the celestial vault will fall;

5 they don't lead a natural and primitive life, as up to now was believed, but have fallen through so defective a corruption from a perfect civilization, in which their ancestors had lived as in their own native society: because to judge a state as wicked as the savage to be natural is not very sensible:

6 it being impossible that Nature, always concerned with the welfare of the animals and above all of man, who it seems we all agree is her principal work, should have destined to man, as if appropriate, required, and adapted to him, a life so wretched and so harsh that he is frightened at the very thought of it.

7 Nor does it seem possible for the true and perfect state of man to be at the end of as long a road as our species seems forced to tread before becoming civilized, where a hundred years are a day as far as results are concerned: so slow is his progress on those paths which lead him from the trees to civilization.

8 Because it would have been unjust and cruel and by no means befitting, for as many human beings as had to be born and die before civilization was attained to have been predestined to unhappiness, not through any vice or guilt of their own, but innocently, through original disposition and their natural fate.

9 Consequently it is believed that the rough and savage life is corruption, not the natural state, and that insulting his destiny man falls here from a great height, I mean from the civilized level, where divine wisdom was careful to place him: because if we don't want to outrage heaven, he is born civilized and later on becomes savage.

10 This conclusion, which however nice will seem to you unusual and strange, derives from no other source but that straightforward and healthy form of reasoning which in the schools is still called *a priori,* beside which every other nowadays appears

vain, which poses as certain some principle and bends and ar-
ranges everything else to fit it.

11 It is assumed for certain that Nature is always concerned with
the well-being of the animals, that she loves them heartily as the
good mother hen does with the chick she has under her wings:
and it being evident that the life mortals lead in the woods is
harsh and wicked in every respect, it is necessarily concluded in
the name of logic that the city came before the citizen.

12 If minds were free and open to what facts and reason could teach
and not inclined to one opinion more than another, if they were
able to call Nature pitiless and deprived of whatsoever sort of
kind feeling and ancient and principal executioner and enemy
of her children,

13 or addressed to any end sooner than to what we call our good or
evil, and to confess that the view of her purpose is removed from
our mortal sight, and even the knowledge of whether or not she
is truly freed of purpose, and if indeed she really has one, what
it is, we would still say with every other age that the citizen came
before the city.

14 Philosophy is nothing but an art which, assigning the reasons for
what man is resolved to believe about whatever issue, as best as
she can fills the papers or the ears sometimes as a school, with
more or less cleverness according to the capacity that the teacher
or author happens to possess.

15 I mean that philosophy which reigns uncontested in our century
and which with relatively little struggle had no less fortune in
the other centuries, except in the one previous to this, when, if
my thought is whole I dare say, each faculty of ours progressed
to those heights from which soon it must incline towards the
bottom. [2]

---

[2] Leopardi reaffirms here his great esteem for the materialistic philosophy
of the eighteenth century.

16   In that age, in spite of a hard struggle, another philosophy was
     seen to reign, before which our age, brave and prompt, drew
     back as soon as she became aware of what displeases her most
     and matters most: that the other was in substance bitter and
     wicked; not that she was really able on her own to prove false
     in her the principles or the premises.

17   But whether or not these[3] were proved to be false or true,
     misshapen or beautiful, their consequences were not those which
     man has decreed to believe in firmly and will believe in firmly as
     long as the stars move from east to west through their usual
     orbit: because it seems that for his own peace he needs such a
     faith in them, whether truth or dreams.

18   And furthermore, because for a long time his mind has been used
     to such a faith, and every faith to which the mind is accustomed
     seems to be produced by an innate conscience: for as habit is
     very easily exchanged with nature, so it easily happens that people
     take their habit for reason.

19   And I believe that learning most of the time is nothing else, if
     one were to consider it seriously, but the perception of foolish
     beliefs contracted by the mind from carrying them around a long
     time and the painful recovery of the knowledge, which age took
     away from us, of the child, who indeed neither knows nor sees
     more than we but does not believe that he sees or knows.

20   But in fact we at once judge every thought to be absurd if it is
     out of the ordinary, and we don't consider that the world and
     truth could be an absurdity to our frail intellect: we cry mystery
     because every human concept still turns out to be a mystery, yet
     we want to fashion the mysteries and the absurdities within our
     brain as we please.

21   Now, my readers, getting down to the point at which, through a
     long and tortuous path always intending, I have arrived, you can

---

[3] Premises.

see by this time how it happens that the very ancient relatives of the mice are portrayed in your imagination just like the people of today, not through deception or foolishness on my part,

22 but due to the fact that our state, not just of men but of every animal that lives anywhere in the air or on the earth, is truly ancient and primitive. Because it would be unjust for the infinite multitude of the animals to be condemned by their very nature to a life deprived of almost every pleasure and full of woe.

23 Consequently all of their species came into the world civilized, each one according to its natural degree, and all of them, through their own fault, fell to the bottom from such a fortunate state, and now they are wretched. And heaven, which had provided well for their needs, has no fault in their miserable state.

24 If the life of the little mouse, who looking around is never sure, who flees and at every quiver is struck with horror, appears to us full of anguish and fear, we must suppose that the misery which the mouse is suffering nowadays, and to which perhaps he was led in part by the events which these papers narrate, is corruption and not his natural state.

25 And perhaps in that time began the dispersion of his race, which, having lost its original and proper home, has been made to wander over the earth, like the Jewish people, who, in exile and scattered, find it hard to adjust to hundreds of places, and re-member the temple of Hierosolyma [4] and the fields of Palestine and weep.

26 But the new master, when he had sworn that he and his heirs would eternally respect the pact, was crowned in a fitting manner, and he put on the mantle of cat fur and grasped the scepter, which was made of gold and in the point of which the world was depicted, because the mouse species believed then to have empire over the entire world.

---

[4] Jerusalem.

27   Cheese with polenta was given to the people and many fountains spouted old wine, while cheerful and thronged together they all cried, "Long live the charter! Long live Bread-Muncher!" [5] so that throughout that mountainous vault was echoed "charter" and "bread," things, for those who know how to administer them, sufficient for the government of educated people. [6]

28   Whether it was his own invention or his subjects', he bore the new title of King of the Mice, not of Rat City, as in the past the bearers of that golden charge had been properly called. A thing very worthy of note, because in practice it makes a lot of difference, though it doesn't appear so, whether one is King of the Mice or of Rat City.

29   I point this out again because whoever doesn't pay attention to this metaphysical discovery could easily be quite mistaken in the chronology and believe that this was the first among those kings to be named Bread-Muncher, when it is clear from books and from coins that there was a Bread-Muncher the Third before this one.

30   First among the kings of the mice, but counting also those of Rat City, if I am not mistaken in my calculation, he was Bread-Muncher the Fourth. If this is not known, the whole chronology can turn topsy-turvy. Therefore, to obviate that, take notice that he was — and the erudites and the philomice note this — Bread-Muncher the First among the kings of the mice, not among the mice kings. [7]

---

[5] Charter: constitution.

[6] That is, it is sufficient art of government for educated people to administer bread and printed lies, provided that the dosage be properly administered.

[7] Leopardi here seems to allude to Louis-Philippe, who called himself King of the French and not King of France, and to Ferdinand IV of Naples, who changed his title to Ferdinand I, King of the two Sicilies. It must be remembered that Leopardi's satire is not limited to the Italians and the Austrians, but is directed at the whole of Europe of the first three decades of the nineteenth century. It is an examination of the present and a revaluation of the past for the sake of finding a better way.

31 The celebration had not yet come to an end when the messenger arrived from the camp, no longer expected, because his long delay had removed every thought of him, nor wished for any longer, because until then dreams were more pleasant than the truth. Dreams were the short leisures and the gaiety, truth what the count was coming to report.

32 As soon as the rumor of his return was spread in Rat City, the concourse of people was everywhere interrupted and the joyful noise quieted. What they had longed for and sighed for just a couple of days before seemed an evil presage, because it awakened to doubts and worries the souls already reassured by oblivion.

33 Quickly the ambassador explained to Bread-Muncher the crab's mood and the harsh laws, and by order of the king he proposed the affair the following day in the greater council. The laws set forth seemed unjust and strange; comments and explanations were made upon them. In the end, however, in order to have peace within and without, it seemed best to consent to everything.

34 The count, with servants and paraphernalia, returned to the camp [8] for the harsh contracts, and signed the agreement according to the terms which you have already heard in my verses. The crab didn't know how to sign the treaty or even how to read it, arts disagreeable to his regions; but a little frog [9] who was then serving as his scribe read it and ratified it with his hand.

35 Swiftly a very cheerful troop of thirty thousand lansquenets moved towards Rat City, at double pay and more than double meals, although the agreement was not yet ratified, and entered the country, jeered before and behind in the streets with the worst insults everyone was able to imagine, and they weren't at all aware of them.

36 They were led into the lofty castle, where, having planted and unfurled their flag, they began to empty pots and barrels, and the

---

[8] The camp of the crabs.

[9] Some commentators have identified this little frog with Cardinal Ruffo.

mice once more hoped for peace. The days and the nights were once again merry and the town, for joy over the newly acquired monarchy, often illuminated both at great expense. [10]

37   But what is more important, it is said that the king devoted himself zealously to making both the state of the people and of the private citizens as prosperous as possible. As soon as Bottom-Licker had returned, he appointed him adviser, secretary of the interior, and chief instrument of the empire in general.

38   The latter turned all of his attention to wiping out ignorance and to the advancement of civilization, knowing that with any other foundation the prosperity of kingdoms does not last and that, when they are civilized and wise, the people themselves know better than anyone else how to procure their own happiness and their own well-being, that they need no favor or gift from the throne but to be free.

39   And he desired for all the people to learn through formal training to read and to count, considering that, I believe, a greater advantage than Henry the Fourth's chicken. Therefore, he had so many schools set up everywhere in the city that in the morning piazzas, porticos, and streets for many days resounded with nothing but A B C.

40   It also pleased him to add more than one teaching post or lectureship to each secondary school, with higher salaries than any professor however stupid ever by chance had. Along with mouse law and natural law, every pre-Justinian law, and civil and criminal law, constitutional law was expounded.

41   And already, owing to the confidence which a proper government produces in the people, the nation was beginning to flourish again with rapid growth of industry. Companies of very rich people sought profit from great expenditures, and each day you could see the place newly embellished with gardens, public baths, and gymnasiums.

---

[10] Because Rat City was underground, it was not reached by the sunlight.

42   New stores and productive factories likewise could be seen going up each day and exposing in great abundance to the passers-by local and imported merchandise, making citizens of foreign conveniences; new theaters assembling the people; here the populace intent on repairing streets and there on laying the foundation of a palace.

43   Meanwhile the city had ratified the agreement with a unanimous vote of approval, and it was expected that the master of the crabs would do the same. Several messengers were already worn out going and coming and nothing yet was concluded, so that in the end some suspicion, albeit confused, was aroused in the hearts of the leaders.

44   Without-Head, the crab king, was held to be the proudest of the princes of that time, a very stubborn and bitter enemy of the mere name of charter or constitution, who would have believed it shameful to divide unreservedly with Jupiter himself the power that was his. If anyone within his kingdom even dreamed of charter, he exercised his wits at punishing him.

45   He made sure that the penalty was inflicted with perfect rigor and that no part of it was left out by people moved to pity, and he remembered the number and the tenor of the blows and the rod prescribed for that purpose. Moreover, the court declared him a good, indeed divine violinist. [11]

46   After concealing the truth for a long time with complicated and vague answers, he sent, when it pleased him to do so, one of his messengers to the captain of those who, admitted without a blow and without casualties, already were openly demanding double pay from the mice. That captain had the highest honors among the speakers of the crab people.

47   So strong in his words that on account of his strong speech he was called Ironed-Mouth. When he arrived at the royal gates he

---

[11] Francis I was also known for his ability to play the violin.

asked for an unusual, private audience. And introduced, he bowed in accordance with the custom of the court, very politely for a crab. Afterwards, reader, he said what, having rested a bit, I shall narrate in the next canto.

CANTO V

1   Sire, he said, because such you must be called on account of the blood you have in your veins, which we know for certain comes into your family from a royal source, and because you were deemed worthy to marry her who alone keeps alive the family of King Ham-Eater, all of the other majestic fruits having fallen;

2   worthy as much as anyone else of a royal throne my lord esteems you in every respect, but, to tell the truth, he believes that the path by which you came to hold the scepter is not good. People who are not qualified to give it properly have elevated you to the well-deserved honors. But, as you well know, to make or to unmake a king never pertained to anyone but a king.

3   If by reason of death the seat which was held legitimately is left vacant, and the succession is not clear through descent or other royal statute or even through a will in one form or another provided by the deceased king, the other kings spontaneously endeavor to support the derelict kingdom.

4   Either a successor who has been unanimously elected by them is given to that seat, or full of honesty these kings divide the deprived state among themselves with equal love, or he who is able to do so first succeeds, usually whoever proves to be the strongest, alleging genealogical reasons, and usually authenticating them with arms. [1]

---

[1] Reference to the War of the Spanish Succession (1700-1714).

5   The subjects have never been seen to give themselves a new king, weighed and examined by them, nor would it be a lesser absurdity, in my opinion, than if some work of our craftsmen, like a pocket watch or something which may be acquired with money, were seen to choose the buyer who would be able to wear and possess it.

6   The people have no right or vote as regards scepters and diadems, which not they but God made, as we all know. On the contrary, even if at times in extreme cases the throne remains deserted or vacant by reason of popular agitation or seeds of anger, or some weariness or other wherefore the monarchy is extinguished,

7   still the other crowns seek a remedy for the people who destroyed it, and try to legitimize almost that bad mood and to rectify the intention, giving them in a benevolent or wicked manner a new master chosen by them; and they never tolerate their being allowed to choose a king on their own. [2]

8   Because even though your people were ordered by Strong-Claw to provide a new king, this did not mean that this one or that should be elected in a definitive manner the new king, but only gave them the task of proposing the most capable of the royal mantle at the feet of the rulers, who would have examined them at their leisure.

9   Now therefore, Sire, having respect for the virtue that dwells manifest in you and above all for those merits that I have already mentioned, by which you and your people are honored, the majesty of my lord not only wants to make up for and amend the defect of the election but also to give you a token perhaps more worthy of his love.

10   Because not only with his royal diploma, which is always valid even if late, and of those whom he calls allies, who will give it readily out of regard for him, will he, placing on your hair the

---

[2] Here the poet probably alludes to recent events in Belgium and Greece.

wreath, render legitimate what is bastard, because legitimacy, a fleeting thing, comes from heaven or returns there in an instant,

11 but he offers you company useful and ready to annul in spite of the mice the intolerable and not very honest pact [3] which the people forced you to accept, to which my lord sees well you were bound by an act very contrary to your will, disgraceful, to tell the truth, and such that it almost completely extinguished the majesty of this throne.

12 Not only will our mighty thirty thousand who in his name hold the castle unite with you in the noble work of restoring luster to your royal headdress, but also the five hundred thousand who are stationed in the frogs' ports, I mean that army already known to you which under Strong-Claw has just camped in those places,

13 and which, because our master wills it, thus halted in neighboring regions waits to see what movement or new thing takes place in your kingdom; as soon as it receives a sign from you, it will set out on the road to the city, where the mice, either having mended their ways or to their own detriment, will quickly go back to serving.

14 When this has been done, the diploma will be sent to you, with the appropriate terms. And a pact between the two kings will be made as both think proper. But the honor which my king enjoys among all the other kings would today be too much diminished if an agreement were confirmed by him that someone else contracted with subject populace.

15 Nor indeed will he stand for your people to boast of having insulted the scepters, and whatever may happen, he will oppose the unbecoming pact which seems to offend all the rulers until it is destroyed and the city returns to what it was before. The captain's oration had this almost hostile conclusion.

---

[3] The constitution.

16   Bread-Muncher, who had heard that it was the crabs' habit to change appearance according to the times and who now saw clear evidence of that, being certain that Without-Head had demanded that the mice immediately elect a king when he was afraid of a more scandalous experience, answered.

17   As soon as he had removed from his heart the suspicion that they might have preferred a free state to any sort of monarchy, and that their example might have engendered in others desire for a similar condition, he condemned the treaties of Strong-Claw and twisted the clear words into inconceivable meanings.

18   He cared very little that the agreement was deprived of the royal seal or that he was not recognized as king of the mice, but that with great surprise he would have seen the castle held by the crab people, who had been able to enter it only by agreement, if he had not known that the rights of nations were denied to these people.

19   And even the common and natural rights, because fraud, perfidy, and whatsoever pure, solemn, and authentic imposture is, against them, a lawful and pious thing, and any foreign or domestic monarchy can with a calm mind oust them, because people and nobody mean the same thing: if you kill them all, you don't kill anyone. [4]

20   As for the proposed business, that he would consult the citizens individually, [5] it not being in his power to take a decision on his own regarding the state, and that he would do what the nation ordered as if it were his own choice, considering it important to observe the constitution since he swore to do so. And having said this, he dismissed him.

21   The next morning he reported everything personally to the general council, and explained and discussed at length the greatness

---

[4] Leopardi continues to expose ironically the theory of monarchy by divine right, according to which the people are of no account.
[5] They would be allowed to vote on the matter.

of the common danger, and repeatedly urged them to find some course, some advice, some suitable measure, almost as if he himself knew a way but did not want to say it.

22 Every breast burned with anger, every face burned, and as often happens after an open insult, which strikes even the coward deep in the heart where certainly the wound hurts, it seemed brave even to the most cowardly to take vengeance for real and not just with words. War was chosen by all and by all it was resolved to die for the constitution.

23 Bread-Muncher commended this unanimous will of his people with much praise, imprecating death upon those beasts, deaf-minded and yet clever at deception; on condition, he said, that no one at variance with his own feelings will follow the words and then the actions of the brave; and he began to make ready troops, arms, and the other things portaining to war.

24 Concerning his true feelings or those closest to the truth, on which every writer is silent, I shall tell you my own opinion as the evil-thinking person I became not very long ago, because through natural disposition I had for a long time believed his intentions to be upright and holy, and it never happened to me to guess this, or to be mistaken when I used the contrary.

25 I say that Bread-Muncher considered it a foolish thing to place his own cause separate from the common cause of the mice in the hands of the crabs, having seen, it may be said, with his own eyes as much treachery gathered in that people as is spread from India to Ethiopia, and being able to think that after the pact they would likewise have gotten rid of him.

26 But he would have desired that the fear of the crabs' war lead the people to be satisfied that the seat given to him was not broken, so that willingly scattering to the wind the fragile charter, without saying a word more, they could have waited to see if it ever pleased the crab king to fulfill his promises.

27 In this way, perhaps within a short time he would have found
himself king without a war and without a pact, freed at one fell
swoop of a double nuisance and with the dynasty well rooted,
and this would not have resulted through any wicked action on
his part, through treason or barratry, nor through his having
violated in any way the oath sworn to the city.

28 Turning these things over in his mind, I believe, he would have
wished the people less heroic. I pass these on to you as my own
conjectures, because history, as I have said, is silent on the matter.
If they seem to you trifles, it is not my intention to belittle his
well-known virtue. Having seen the will of his people, he prepared
for war with great ardor as though it were the best thing to do.

29 You would have heard all the orators thundering war in all the
assemblies, Leonidas, Themistocles, Cimon, Mucius Scaevola,
the dictator Fabius, Decius, Aristides, Codrus, Scipio,[6] and
similar heroes of their ancestors often named in the councils
and all day long circulating on the mouths of the populace.

---

[6] We have preferred the singular forms of these names (Leopardi gives
them in the plural), since it would sound awkward in English to say "Aristi-
deses" and "Themistocleses." The concept, however, remains clear: Leopardi
means "men of this sort." Leonidas is the famous hero of Thermopylae
(480 B. C.); Themistocles is the great Athenian statesman and soldier
(d. 449 B. C.), the creator of the Athenian naval policy and the rival of
Aristides; Cimon, a renowned Athenian general statesman (502-449 B. C.);
Caius Mucius Scaevola (who lived about 500 B. C.) was a courageous
Roman soldier who, condemned to be burned for attempting to kill Porsena,
king of the Etruscan town of Clusium, showed his contempt for torture by
thrusting his right hand into the flames, and was pardoned for his heroic
act. Fabius was the name of an important Roman family which gave
various illustrious political figures, among whom Quintus Fabius Maximus
Pullianus and Quintus Fabius Maximus Verruculus, who were several times
consul; the latter was appointed dictator during the Second Punic War.
Decius, Publius Decius Mus, another prominent Roman family, gave three
noble patriots, a grandfather, a son, and a grandson, who lived in the
fourth and third centuries B. C. Codrus was the last king of Athens
(d. 1066 B. C.), since no one else was deemed worthy to succeed him. Aristides,
the great Greek statesman and general and the rival of Themistocles, was
nicknamed "the Just." Named Scipio were Publius Cornelius Scipio Africanus
(237-183 B. C.), one of the most famous Roman generals, who defeated
Hannibal at Zama in 202 B. C., and Scipio Africanus Emilianus (185-129
B. C.), the adopted grandson of "the Elder," also a general and consul,
who burned Carthage, thereby ending the Third Punic War (149-146 B. C.).

30 Songs and ditties that the people took delight in singing, sounding war, all the factories repeating war, each one in its own way with its own effect. Throughout all the forges spears were flashing, arms for the head, arms for the breast, and in all the songs loud threats could be heard, and patriotic fervor and boasts.

31 The first act of war, Chunk-Stealer moving the citizens to such labor, was to close with towers and fences all the confines of the castle occupied by the enemy, from where they could at any moment from the open height hurl themselves down on their neighbors and bring sudden tempest and war on the land.

32 Afterwards it was debated whether it would be the best thing to oppose half-way the major nerve of the crab army, which by then would come from beyond like a swift and lofty torrent, or with ample provisions and the gates closed, to scoff at their fury from inside the city. The old people liked the latter idea, but to the dandies of the country the former seemed glorious.

33 As Ajax, that day when the Greek troops, who were fighting as hard as they could to preserve Patrocles for the funeral services, were surrounded with darkness by Jupiter, implored the god to grant sight to the eyes of the Achaeans' sons, to bring back the day, and then, if he wanted, to destroy them in the open splendor, [7]

34 so those brave ones begged the popular council to let the valor of their right hands shine clearly before all eyes in the bright countryside and not let their peril remain hidden in the dark bosom of that mountainous cave. The difficult sentence won, and it was resolved to face the crabs outside.

35 And already from the realms sweet to remember of the frog friends, who had had to lodge them very well up to that time, those with the stony crust, Strong-Claw and his faithful soldiers, were moving by that will which forces every will, of their master

---

[7] Episode narrated in Homer's *Iliad,* Book XVII.

and king, who had ordered the commander to move immediately on Rat City.

36   From the other direction, horrible in appearance, the phalanx of citizens which numbered close to a million and a half infantrymen was moving out of Rat City. Xerxes did not cross into Europe with so many when the sea was crossed on foot. [8] Every path was covered so far that the gaze was lost in the black.

37   They had come to the place where Looker-Around put an end to the others' flight, a pleasant and cheerful place with its little meadows and hills and stillness. It was that time of day when the morning hours yield the paths of the world to noon, when very far away a little cloud seemed to rise in front of the army.

38   A little cloud which was growing little by little with such astonishing swiftness that it seemed bound to cover and darken the whole plain within a short time, like fog sometimes, which is formed far off in a low valley by a river or marsh, and advances by puffs and little by little with its darkness swallows up fields and villages.

39   The chiefs easily understood what was indicated by the white cloud, which was produced by the march of the animals who were coming as adversaries of the mixed kingdom. [9] Therefore it clearly seemed to the generals time to prove their talent, and having stopped here, with great skill they drew up the brave troops in battle array.

40   They positioned the extreme right wing of the squadron near the lake that I mentioned above, which now clear and shining in the bright daylight scattered the rays of the midday sun, the other on the high, steep knoll that I also described above, and they had their people occupy all the narrow, woody, and high places in the area.

---

[8] Reference to the crossing of the Hellespont by Xerxes and his army by means of a bridge made of boats tied together (480 B. C.) during the war against the Greeks.

[9] Constitutional monarchy.

41 Already through the moving cloud of dust could be discerned the hard crab people, who quietly and without noise were coming secure in their gravity. Here may the matter lift my song and render it clear if before it was obscure! Here I would willingly invoke the muse except that it is no longer customary to invoke her.

42 The two phalanxes were face to face, already spread out and about to fight, when from all over the plain, from all over the mountain the mouse people took flight. How, I don't know, but neither stream, fountain, cliff, nor forest stopped their course. They would still be fleeing, I believe, if flight kept fugitives alive so long.

43 They fled like the wind, like lightning as far as my story subsequently narrates. Of them all only Chunk-Stealer remained on the deserted field, as straight as a cypress, motionless, not thinking it allowed a citizen to seek his safety after the act of his people, after the disgrace of which that day was only the beginning for the mice.

44 When they turned against him, the enemy felt the Herculean power of his arm. Though hard and thick, the shell was not strong enough to save them from it. Every cleaving blow of that sword, falling, broke it, and made the bones creak, and cut off the claws, and covered the ground with a half-dead and gelid multitude.

45 Thus fighting alone against an infinite number he remained as long as there was light. When the sun had descended to other shores, feeling his mortal body afflicted and weary, his chest and side wounded and lacerated all over by very sharp pains, and no longer able to hold up the shield, on which a horrible and dense mass of spears and various arms were nailed,

46 he threw it far away, where he felt the enemy the thickest. Many remained mangled and crushed from it, others who had been squashed dirtied the plain. After he had gathered his last strength,

he never rested his hand from fighting until, the veil of night having thickened, he fell, but the sky did not see his fall.

47   Noble valor, whenever it perceives you my spirit, as at a happy event, rejoices: nor does it believe that you should be scorned even if you are nourished and cultivated in mice. Before your beauty, which exceeds all others, whether renowned or hidden it finds you, my spirit always bows down; and not only when you are true and real, but even imagined, it is warmed by you.

48   Ah! but where are you? Always dreamed of or sham? Did no one ever see you real? Or were you indeed extinguished along with the mice, and no longer your beauty smiles among us? Ah! if you were not vainly depicted with laurels, and did not perish with Theseus or Alcides, [10] certainly from then on your smile was each day more rare and less beautiful.

---

[10] Theseus, the famous son of the king of Athens, killed the Minotaur. Alcides is another name for Hercules, who was the grandson of Alcaeus.

CANTO VI

1   The inviolate troops crowded the four gates of Rat City, goal of their flight. Not only had the strong crab people not been able to wound them, they had not even been able to see them well. Caesar, who saw and conquered, was in my opinion less formidable than Strong-Claw, who without seeing could with his soldiers easily put to rout three times as many.

2   As soon as the army had returned home safe and sound — if the flight wasn't mortal to a few — the gates of their den were closed with diligence equal to the fear. And any animal's every effort to get in there would have been for a long time vain, so that Strong-Claw, who had arrived there right away, would have spent many years at this,

3   except that those who through wicked deceit were lords of the castle and who now raising many torches to the wind were sitting up there on top as scouts, having seen the people moving about in a state of agitation and those who were outside return inside, guessed what was going on and, made bold, forced the ill-guarded barricades.

4   And having overrun the land with blood and terror, they opened the gates to their companions, who, as a tiger breaks loose from the cage or as a horrid snake hurls itself from a branch, rushed inside and without a blow immediately filled the whole place. You can feel in your heart the plundering, the destruction of a victorious enemy rabble.

5 For several days the conquered city was put under martial law,
   with Strong-Claw in command, or to tell the truth that little frog
   he had with him just for the purpose of revealing to him in part
   on the days when mail arrived the alphabetic mystery, and whenever there was need of the art of understanding or speaking by
   means of paper.

6 Soon every act, every sign, insignia, or motto of mixed monarchy
   was cast to the winds, razed, cut down, transformed, or smashed.
   Whoever spoke of constitution or parliament was led to prison by
   the lansquenets, who without understanding a single word more
   of the mouse language were marvelously learned in that family of
   words.

7 Bottom-Licker, who was known for his true love of country and
   of civil progress, not only was deprived of the office and power
   granted to him by the king, but was banished entirely from
   the court and the administration through the expressed will of
   Without-Head, and he began to spend his days and seasons among
   the master-spies.

8 In my opinion the crabs would have willingly toppled Bread-
   Muncher from the throne. But since they could not easily find
   anyone else who owing to his blood was so fit to reign, having
   devoted much thought to the matter, the victorious king judged
   it best to pardon him and call him king without any other contract;
   if he was not by right, he was at least by fact.

9 But with the title and the appearance of ambassador he sent to
   him Baron Crooked-Walker, [1] a great meddler and a great swind-
   ler and learned and shrewd in every royal matter, who through
   cunning and force quicky succeeded in arranging for the kingdom
   to be governed as he advised, for neither branch nor leaf to
   move there against his will.

---

[1] Crooked-Walker is commonly identified with Prince Metternich (1773-
1859), the famous Austrian diplomat who was mainly responsible for shaping
the conservative and repressive politics of Europe after the Congress of
Vienna.

10 By his order the reading room was closed as well as the schools that the count had established, as I said above, and by his will it was forbidden to the people to be instructed in letters without obtaining a special permit for that: because the crab kings were never tired of opposing the A B C's.

11 Hence their realms were truly the dark kingdoms of the upper world. And this was rightly so, because clearly they had to see that the pride in which their house was eminent above all others had nowhere but the ignorance of others on which to brood: because once this was removed, they had no other shade from contempt.

12 I omit many, many other dispositions of the wise ambassador, and I shall only say that evidence of the excellence of his measures was industry slackening throughout the kingdom, usury increasing, people becoming poor, every talent hiding from the sun, only fools or known and manifest scoundrels seeking and transacting civil affairs.

13 The people, humilited and infiltrated with spies, every day becoming worse in their habits, resorting to deceits and lies, becoming shameless and traitorous; the streets unsafe from thieves, all through the city as well as outside; with gold and faith in flight, law-suits making their entrance and lawyers going around fat and in great numbers.

14 As soon as the orator to whom the government of the mice was entrusted by the king of the crabs had arrived, Strong-Claw was enjoined to leave with his soldiers. But increased by this very one to exactly one hundred thousand, the crowd barely fit into the castle; the rest returned with Strong-Claw to their holes to triumph over mice and frogs.

15 Then there was born among the mice a madness more worthy of laughter than of pity, a faction which went back and forth plotting at leisure in the streets, speaking with force and charm

of patriotism, honor, and freedom, each one of them resolved, if it came to action, to flee as they had done before, [2]

16 and certain, as for himself, that not even with his finger or with his tail would he touch lansquenets. Also it pleased the youth especially to receive or to give with an unwincing face stinging invitation to future slaughters, because it was fashionable to conspire, and projecting dangers and destruction of the city served them as a pastime.

17 They let the hair of the muzzle and the whiskers grow thick and excessively long, hoping, because hair promises boldness, to be able to frighten at least the mice. Every day they showed up in the coffeehouses, thoughtful, with the newspapers in their hands, speaking of their conspiracy, and then in the evening they went around in groups singing suspicious songs.

18 Crooked-Walker laughed through and through at such comedies and willingly allowed this comfort to the mice, that openly and to his knowledge, decreeing him now captured, now dead, they might conspire against him entire lustrums; but later on he would not stand for the count to become head and source of these plots.

19 The young rowdies flocking around him offered themselves ready to die for the country; and his house was never empty day or night of some of these. Because people, though learned and wise and of honest deeds and intentions, are always eager to command others, and more so if at some time in the past they had such satisfaction,

20 and urged also by the country's name and by that true love of which he was always a model, he brought himself to give, if not his whole feeling, at least a receptive ear to the sweet sound

---

[2] Here and in the following stanzas we have a flavorful satire of the Carbonari, the clandestine Italian patriotic groups which organized, with little success, various conspiracies against the Austrian regime between 1820 and 1831.

that was boasting of his return to office and the country's return to its former honor and rank, and was soliciting his heart with hope.

21   The ambassador still didn't fear much the distant longings of the count, yet as it was necessary to surround him with many well-paid spies, one day he decided to direct that money to other purposes and to free himself of that nuisance, and politely and in the form of advice he forced the count to go off into exile.

22   A pilgrim about the earth, the illustrious mouse saw many peoples, nations, and customs; he went to as many animals as Aesop later told of, crossing seas and rivers, keeping his eyes always fixed on one goal: to bring, as we say, greater light to his people and, if it should be granted to him, to find help for their sorrowful state.

23   As an exile and as someone who was disagreeable to the crab king and to Baron Crooked-Walker and loved the alphabet and the common people, many courts regarded him with a suspicious eye. Several others were less miserly with him, several ministers and kings gave him generous comfort of promises, and satisfied, he went on his way with that wind.

24   One autumn night, since he traveled a lot at night, as is customary with mice, a storm gathered over his head obscured every glimmer of the stars; an icy cloud twisted into a cyclone filled the shores with sandy foam and made the path so indiscernible from the fields that it became impossible to follow it.

25   Rushing with fury the wind broke off the branches and uprooted the trees, and from time to time the lightning crashing down split nearby cliffs and oak-trees with a tremendous sound, which every summit and valley echoed with a roar, and with such a refulgence that it seemed all of a sudden to fill the whole place with fire.

26   Having keen sight and seeing things with precision in the dark were of no use to the count, because he had very soon lost the road, and he found himself separated from his followers. He was

swimming or sliding at every point through the countryside, now become a lake. Several times he almost drowned, and he lifted his eyes imploring to heaven.

27   The wind, constantly changing direction, pushed him back and forth several times, now and then turned him upside down and soaked his tail, his back, and his hair in the icy humor, and several times, to tell the truth, that apparatus of dreadful threats made his heart contract, because seldom fear, but often terror overcomes the feelings of the wise.

28   Dogs, sheep, and oxen that were outside, scattered on the plain or up the mountains, were furiously swept away by the sudden currents rolling into the distance, as far as the rivers, as far as the ocean, leaving the poor shepherd destitute. Fortune and the light weight of his limbs saved the count from rolling to the bottom.

29   The storm had already ceased and one by one the stars, still almost timid and insecure and moist from the storm, seemed to peep through the dark clouds. But all around, the valleys and the plains were flooded, and like an empty little boat amid the waves, without any path the mouse was swimming this way and that.

30   And in his heart the anguish of the present state had taken the place of the terror. Without any knowledge of the place, he was alone, already tired, and soaking wet. A cold little wind, armed with points and knives, had started from the north, and blowing, struck him everywhere and seemed to cut him to the quick and shred him.

31   So that if he should not find any hole or cover to escape the water and the intense cold and should have to spend without shelter the night, which had not yet half-way climbed the sky, he really felt that before dawn he would lose his skin. Thinking about that and changing his direction at every moment, he saw very far away a small light,

32   which among the dripping hedges and trees now appeared to him and now seemed to have fled. But proceeding ahead he well realized that it was stationary and fixed, and he decided to propose that signal to his wandering steps, or rather to his swimming, and thus having waded more than a mile, he found himself in front of a palace.

33   It was large, and beautiful beyond measure, with loggias all around and balconies, and in front of it there could be heard through the dark air two fountains raining with everlasting sounds. The mouse saw that it had the size and shape of human dwellings: from the light which was coming from a window it also appeared to be inhabited.

34   Therefore with care and effort the weary mouse searched it outside in every angle, to see if he could find a new or ancient crack where he could rest awhile, our species not being very friendly to his even as far back as the period I celebrate in these verses. But although he tried very hard he found neither crack nor hole in those walls.

35   This will seem strange to you, but certainly purposeful fate led him there to the place you are going to hear about. Because seeing by then death close by, which Cesari called "sending for the priest," [3] and feeling himself doomed to die of every evil except thirst if he stayed outside any longer, the count determined to change dangers, to be daring and to knock.

36   When he had pulled himself to the door and taken a pebble, he struck several blows as hard as he could. Suddenly from a balcony a man peeped out and looked, but he didn't see anyone. The one who was knocking was too small, nor easy to see through the

---

[3] Antonio Cesari (Verona, 1760-1828, Ravenna), a priest and a renowned scholar in his time, was considered the principal exponent of "purism" in the Italian language, that is, the return to the literary language of the fourteenth century (chiefly the language of Dante, Petrarch, and Boccaccio), and fought the corruption of foreign influence, especially of French. Cesari's expression, "sending for the priest," is presented ironically as an example of the priest's pedantry and affectation.

darkness. He pushed the shutters to again, and shortly afterwards there the light knocking was as before.

37 This time the inhabitant of the solitary abode drew out a lighted lamp, stuck his head out, and staring attentively towards the door, saw before it the mouse who with his outstretched paw was using the pebble as a hammer. You probably think that he put the cat out, but he immediately went down to open,

38 and in a very courteous manner he ushered the pilgrim into gilded rooms, speaking the true and natural language of the species and country of the mice. And having seen him so sadly dressed and his teeth chattering from the cold outside, he led him to a bath, where he himself washed the mud off him and warmed him.

39 When he had done this, he brought him a meal fit for a king, of walnuts and dried figs, Parmesan cheese, one of those well-aged ones, slices of bacon and sweetmeats and cakes, everything of such a savor that to the count every meal he had had in court seemed like straw and sticks. After he had eaten his supper, he asked him his name, where he came from, and how.

40 And like Aeneas in the Libyan halls [4] the pilgrim began to tell his story. The other was seated in front of him on a high-backed chair, and he on a small table, gesticulating with two paws, and there was hanging from his neck a little cordon given to him as a token of honor by the late King Ham-Eater, which with difficulty he had rescued from the waves.

41 And concisely he told from the beginning of his ancestry, his parents, and his own condition. Then getting down to the offices he had held, he began to speak of his people; he told of the frogs and the mood of the citizens, the charter, and the wicked and

---

[4] Reference to the beginning of Book II of Virgil's *Aenead,* where Aeneas, at the invitation of Queen Dido, begins to narrate his various adventures.

tyrannical crab, and, lowering his eyes, he related the two flights, and the plots, and the ignoble exile.

42 And at the end, as was his custom, [5] he recounted the hopes and the promises, authentic and expressed, which he had received from more than one possible ally, and he begged the host to join the others in giving aid to the mice in any way he could. The latter offered rare poisons of herbs, active and quick, but the count refused them,

43 saying that, apart from the fact that such a remedy could not easily be put to work, it would be quite useless to that end which he placed above every other, of restoring the honor of his people, from which one who uses wicked artifices strays afar. The other praised his words and promised him that before he waked up

44 he would have thought intently about the case in order to find, if he could, some solution. It was already dawning in the east, the gleam of many stars had disappeared, and the sky all clear and translucent promised a beautiful day to follow. The ground was almost clear of the waters and the north wind had died down.

45 The host led the count to a balcony, showing him the peaceful and calm weather. The silence was broken only by the two fountains nearby, and far away by the cricket. A few rare flashes of lightning over the mountain recalled the storm to the one who had endured it. Then he guided him to a well-prepared bed and for the time being took leave of him.

---

[5] The count had already told his story at other courts.

CANTO VII

1   I forgot to add in the last canto that the mouse also asked the unknown one his name and state, why he was so kind to a wandering mouse, and from what books or through what enchantment he had learned the voices of the mice. He told him part of it, and the rest he said he would tell more leisurely the next day.

2   Daedalus was his name, and in skill he was like the one who built the labyrinth. According to ancient documents it was rumored or presumed that he was the same one. If the reason of the times [1] separates them, I don't want to be accused of anachronism. I don't know the age of Crete or of Minos: Niebuhr would tell of it if he were alive. [2]

3   Very ancient, it is clear, was the epoch of our man. However, readers, I declare and even protest that the Daedalus so famous nowadays perhaps and probably was not the one about whom I am going to talk, but how much more modern I couldn't say. And without further delay my song returns to its path.

---

[1] The chronology.

[2] Berthold Georg Niebuhr (Copenhagen, 1776-1831, Bonn), German historian whose lessons in archeology at the University of Berlin and afterwards at Bonn were very renowned throughout Europe. His most important work, *Romische Geschichte* (1911-1912), laid down the foundation for the critical historiography of Rome. From 1816 to 1823 he served as Prussian ambassador to Rome and had the occasion to meet Leopardi. He was one of the first to acknowledge the importance of Leopardi as an erudite and philologist. The tone here is rather ambiguous, so it is difficult to say whether the poet is paying a compliment or is being ironic.

4   The Daedalus who gave lodging to the mouse was left heir to a rich and noble condition by those who generated him; and bored, I don't know for what reason, with men, who nevertheless — if one looks at it in a straightforward manner — are in general very fine persons, he had retired in solitude to the country to lead a free and calm life.

5   Then, because he had seen the sun more than four hours high, he announced to the traveler, who had been sleeping since dawn with great relish, that the morning was well advanced; and after he had gotten up he led him to a place where morocco in various colors glistened amid the gold, in the study, that is, which all around was adorned with precious books.

6   There he showed him many volumes of ancient and modern mice authors: *The Frenzies* of the great Perfume-Sniffer; *The Trap*, tragedy in twenty acts; *Rat City before the Use of Salted Meats*; the *Acts of the Academy of the Sleepers*; *The Friend of the Famished*; and a canticle in folio for a royal birth.

7   Furthermore, he showed him the grammar and the dictionary of the mouse language and several other books necessary for the correct practice of that tongue, which with the somewhat varied use of the verbs was sister to the Slavonian languages. Then, having gotten him to sit down, he seated himself and started a long discourse.

8   And he told how, having chosen that retreat when he was scarcely out of puberty, he had in that leisure taken such a delight in the physical and mechanical sciences that through them he had put into effect diverse and unusual things, and later on traveling through many countries he had made many new discoveries.

9   And having become highly expert in the history which is called natural, being already from the beginning certain of the civilized state of every animal, [8] he had discovered the languages of many,

---

[8] That is to say, of the fact that every animal, being rational, had a civilization of its own.

some by listening intently, others through books he had found; so that to as many animals as happened to come before him

10   he was, as to his fellow-men, as to companions, always courteous in every way possible. But after he had thus learned the languages of many kinds of animals from many places and hence understood the most hidden qualities of the weakest and of the strongest, a desire which had pursued him for many years had begun to grow in his heart.

11   A compelling desire to find, by going all over the world, through some outward sign the underworld of the animals, as others [4] searching discovered ours; that is to say, that place where after death lived eternally the ego of the animals, [5] which seemed to him demonstrated by common sense to be eternal like ours.

12   Because, he said, whoever doesn't want to close his eyes to the sun or deny his conscience and lie to himself must be certain that from the intelligence of the beasts to that of human progeny the difference is of from less to more, not of the sort that if one rejects the matter, the other admits it. [6]

13   For certainly if I am allowed by right reasoning to consider the ego of the mouse a flimsy thing, or of the dog, or of any other mortal who clearly feels and thinks, I don't see why ours may not be just like these; and if the mouse or the dog doesn't really think or feel, I am allowed to doubt about my own feeling and thinking.

14   He spoke in that manner. But it seems to me that two things, which it is nice to put together, prove more than anything else and almost as if it were engraved that the human mind believes what it has established as certain to such a degree that reason, force, or party can't dissuade it from that belief: one, that while without any doubt everyone assents to the dogma of Copernicus, [7]

---

[4] Orpheus, Theseus, Hercules, Aeneas, etc.

[5] Allusion to the German philosophy of the ego, which was becoming popular in Italy and especially in Neapolitan circles.

[6] The difference is not of the sort that if the matter in question, intelligence, is excluded in one (beast or man), it can subsist in the other.

[7] The theory of the heliocentric system.

15 all the nations and schools are not, however, any less certain and persuaded that man, in short, without peers at his side sits as lord of the created mass, [8] nor are the ancient fables, which picture the gods participating in our life and customs out of love for us, repeated in a less jocular and candid manner.

16 Two, that he who proceeds to inquire into the mysterious essence of the human mind is seen for the most part to leave aside completely, with impudent dissimulation and dishonesty, the question of the animals, [9] as if it were alien to his own, and he doesn't care at all to define his own in such a way that it is absurd to the other.

17 But let's take leave of the others, [10] ahead of whom, for good sense, I place even the modern mice. Let's return to Daedalus and to the intense desire which moved him to seek over all the earth and the immense ocean, as later on the knights-errant did for their beloved ladies, the abode in which the dead animals were still alive.

18 At last he truly found it and saw with his own eyes many naked souls of animals, I mean freed from those bodies that on earth they had worn as veils, although they still seemed to be wrapped up in them; in what way, I couldn't say, but whoever has seen spirits and naked souls in person knows that they always have the appearance of bodies.

19 Therefore, Daedalus offered to lead the traveler to the immortal residence of the deceased mice so that he might consult them about Rat City and the destiny of his people; because we know that every mortal, when he dies, becomes almost prophetic and, whatever he was before, becomes so learned and wise that he surpasses every living being.

---

[8] In several of the *Operette morali*, and most specifically in the *operetta* entitled *Copernicus*, Leopardi had already ridiculed the idea of man as the center of the universe.

[9] That is, whether or not they have a soul.

[10] Those who deny that the animals have a soul.

20 At first this undertaking seemed to the count strange and arduous and full of terror. Orpheus, Theseus, Psyche, Hercules, and Aeneas had not yet made such a descent, of which later on they boasted, and perhaps one of them had learned the art from mice or moles. Daedalus admonished him that the brave fear little the living and not at all the dead.

21 And having easily encouraged him and persuaded him to engage in the undertaking, and having comforted him with some of the foods for which mice are greedy, he equipped him on both sides with little wings. I can't say any more; the story doesn't say a word about what the mechanism was made of, or about the gears, or about the contrivance which made it work.

22 The result clearly proved that this unusual load of wings did not have the defect of those with which Icarus, flying, named the sea: of those which, let it be said incidentally, failed on account of the heat, I don't know how, because in the upper region of the sky it is usually not the heat which is in excess but the cold. [11]

23 Daedalus, I mean our Daedalus, put on wings adjusted to human size. It is not the case to doubt these things, even though they may be of a rather strange sort. We hear, among many things that the age concealed, Father Lana's machine praised, [12] and the aerostatic balloon is believed not through hearsay but because it is seen.

---

[11] Icarus, son of Daedalus, with whom he escaped from the labyrinth by means of wings attached with wax. Flying too close to the sun, so that the wax melted and the wings came off, Icarus fell into the sea which, after him, was called the Icarian Sea (the part of the Aegean Sea lying between Asia Minor and the islands of Patmos and Leros).

[12] Francesco Lana, Conte de' Terzi (Brescia, 1631-1687), Jesuit mathematician and naturalist, who, after a period of literary activity, dedicated himself exclusively to the natural sciences and attracted attention with his plans for building flying machines with static support, producing the vacuum inside large spheres of copper thick enough to resist external atmospheric pressure. The Moroncini edition erroneously reads "Rana," a mistake which the editor himself corrects on page 183.

24 Thus when both had put wings on their backs and had tried out and shaken the new load, up over the terraces of the solitary dwelling they took the same paths which the birds had for their own. Daedalus looked just like a big bird, the one beside him just like a bat; they flew a vast distance, and saw from up high infinite peaks and seas and shores.

25 They saw cities whose appearance and very memory are covered with clods of earth. They saw fields and dense forests and muddy and soft beds of marshy waters which later on were the chosen sites of other cities, which also flourished, which time also destroyed; and now of what they were remains likewise perishable renown.

26 Troy did not exist in that time, nor those who leveled her to the ground, Argos and Mycenae; nor the two rivals, sisters of honor but not of fortune, Sparta and Messene; nor yet existed that other one who later on was to bore the stars with her fame, Athens: empty was the port [13] and empty the place [14] where today pilgrims bow down before the mutilated Parthenon.

27 Nearby the Ganges and the Indus, lofty walls and nations were little by little appearing. In China, near and far in the pure sunlight were shining pagodas and canals running in every direction through the green plain, which, crowded with cities and people, was teeming with commerce and dancing.

28 The Tower of Babel stamped with its immense shadow the barren waste land; and the pyramids on both sides [15] pressed the soil born of the waters. Italy was sparsely inhabited in that time, Italy, which at the end of admirable antiquity comes last in years, and for virtue wins first honors.

29 She was all strewn with burning volcanoes and reduced to ashes on both sides. The Apennines smoked frequently then as Vesuvius

---

[13] Piraeus.
[14] The Acropolis.
[15] Of the Nile.

and Mongibello [16] do now, and fiery torrents of molten rock were a scourge to the Tuscan sea and to the Adriatic; the Alps were smoking, and flames and red hot sand furrowed the snowy ridge.

30   The two flying travelers couldn't raise their wings high enough to keep ashes and even little stones from striking their limbs and their clothes; like towering pines such deluges surged from the loftiest summits towards the eternal seats, darkening the day high all around on earth and on sea.

31   One could hear the mountains thunder and now the Illyrian shore [17] and now the Sardinian resound; not yet, as now, was the Venetian and Lombard plain festive, nor were there then so many lakes, nor did Larius [18] and Garda embellish it with their shores: it was bare and without any amenity, and horrible and dark from hardened lava.

32   Over the hills where Rome now dwells a few solitary horses grazed, wandering in the very bright sunshine which gilds that place proud above all others in the world. Still the daring prow did not guide the pale navigator through the gorge of Scylla, [19] since the traveler came overland by way of Calabria to the Sicilian soil.

33   On the other side, joined to that of Gades, [20] was the shore where later Carthage was born, and already from time to time Phoenician ships could be sighted here and there on the waters. Also visible above the ocean was that vast land, called Atlantis, which later on lay submerged within it, and whose inconstant fame now speaks and wanders.

34   Through her one had easier access then to the shores of that other hemisphere than through the arctic snows and through the polar dawn which flares up in a malign and black sky, and not so full

---

[16] Etna.

[17] Dalmatia.

[18] Lake Como.

[19] Strait of Messina, between Scylla and Carybdis.

[20] Territory of Cadiz, in Spain, which was joined to Morocco, where later Carthage was built.

of dangers as now, cleaving straight through the entire ocean. Among others Plato spoke of her, and the voyage of the mouse is witness of it.

35 Everywhere gigantic beasts, much bigger than Indian elephants or any other beast of enormous size, could be seen moving about or resting on the vegetation. From above they looked like hills wandering around or rising in the middle of the plain. The seeds of such animals, as you know, have been extinct for a long time.

36 Schools and museums are in the habit of conserving, as relics of then, their unearthed bones. The humble rock which covered the city of the mice was recognized again by our birds, [21] and the flying exile, full of pity, looked at it four times and six from up high and, sighing, turned back and lamented his banishment.

37 At last, after flying and seeing so much that it could not be followed with words, the pair of whom I sing discovered a sea which appeared boundless. Perhaps it was the one to which someone who later ploughed it attributed the glory of peace, still called by many meridian, the widest ocean of all. [22]

38 In the midst of the brilliant plain they saw a trace of a dark stain, as this or that shadow on the silver moon appears to the sight, though less dark. And there, directing their flight into the pure air that struck the vast lagoon of the sea, they saw, motionless and, as it were, fixed, a putrid and thick fog stagnating.

39 As a flock of sparrows or partridges which alights on some villa to peck appears to the herder who up the slopes is grazing the goats in the midday sun, so from up high to the two flying friends appeared that eternal fog, indeed night which distills there, in which was enveloped or rather buried an island.

40 This island rose very high above the sea on all sides, with such shores and such precipitous reefs around them and so many very

---

[21] Daedalus and the count.
[22] Pacific Ocean.

deep chasms where with such fury, with such barking the waves pounded and broke, that neither swimmer nor ship had ever hoped even to approach that place.

41   Only the region of the wind could provide a route to the filthy shore. [23] But fright and a stench that issued from the fog drove away the birds. However, these things were no obstacle to our travelers, whose flight terminated there, since that eternal funeral pavilion covered the general underworld of the animals.

42   There, breaking through the wild night, the weary flyers lowered their wings and trod on that land which swallows up the pure and simple ego of every animal, and sat down on the steep banks where no other mortal ever set foot, lifting their eyes towards the deadly mountain which filled the middle of the barren country.

43   That mountain of an immortal, thick, and heavy metal erected its cloudy peak, much blacker than Mount Etna appears up close with overflowed lava, rounded and smooth, and among those hollow shades it seemed like a sepulchral monument: some dream by chance created for us such supernatural spectacles.

44   The mountain was more than a hundred miles around and all around at its roots there were openings astonishingly different one from another in size but not in function. Every family of the deceased animals, from the whales down to the small earthworms, to the fleas, to the insects with which the humors of other animals are filled inside and out,

45   microscopic or even completely hidden to the human eye however well equipped, has here its opening. And those orifices are arranged so that the smaller ones are placed beside the larger ones in order of size. The first is of the biggest whale and is enormous, and gradually descending, the eye sharpens in vain on the last ones.

46   These are doors to as many infernos, which to as many species of animals are permanent and eternal shelters of the souls which

---

[23] It could be approached only from the sky.

have lost their bodies. There, consequently, from all the outer shores spirits of every kind came grazing the air, intent and silent, and each one took that opening which pertained to its species.

47 Deer, buffaloes, monkeys, bears, and horses, oysters, cuttlefish, mullets, and sea-perches, geese, ostriches, peacocks, and parrots, vipers and maggots and little snails, forms crowded together through the airways filled every corner of the dark place, because flight too is a characteristic virtue of the souls naked of their limbs.

48 Daedalus and the count easily discerned here those forms which they had not seen in the sunlight, though behind them, beside them, and in front of them there had always been quite a few mingled in their flight, since from every valley, hill, forest, or fountain, wretched souls go through the sky at every moment towards that place which eternal fate destined as their seat after death.

49 But as the fire-fly lights up only in the darkness and those figures which the magic lantern depicts disappear in the daylight, so the minds attenuated and pure of that veil which constrains them while they are living, are by nature wont to disappear in excessive light and to appear only in the dark.

50 And for this reason, perhaps, it happens that buried people are in the habit of appearing at night and that, except on rare occasions, visions are ordinarily excluded from the daytime. Some people are of the opinion that human souls set free from their bodies are also shut up in one of these infernos, put there like the others in that place which their size requires.

51 And that Virgil and all those who gave to the human seed a refuge apart told fables following Homer and the style and art of the poets, most of the mortal kind being, in truth, more prolific than man. [24] As for myself, I am not intervening in this matter: therefore I hasten to continue the story.

---

[24] That is, it is obvious that man, less prolific and therefore less numerous than the other animals, cannot have a hell separate from that of the other animals, as poets, following the fantasy of Homer, continued to narrate.

CANTO VIII

1 The reason why the dead had their lodging underground is not entirely known to me. I can well understand about the bodies, because the inanimate and motionless remains return to the earth. But I don't quite know why the immortal spirit which breaks loose from the body also hits bottom. Even if other authorities were not available, the count's story would affirm that to be true.

2 Astonished, the good Bottom-Licker remained staring for a long time at the novelty of the infernal residence, and was forgetting the motive of his journey and the return. But Daedalus shook him, and after they had gone part way round the mountain, they discovered the opening there where in swarms the souls [1] of the deceased mice assembled.

3 Before the unamiable threshold the two living beings had to separate, because Daedalus, although he wanted to, could not enter among the dead mice, not only living but even if he went among the dead people as a naked soul: because not even half the figure of man, dead or alive, fits through that door.

4 The strong and wise man had indeed visited infernos of his own stature and larger, and having seen them to be, except in size, similar among themselves, he had foretold to the mouse every risk of that journey, which he now retold, and he encouraged him, and having placed him within the everlasting horror, he remained outside to wait for him.

---

[1] Translated literally, *forms* (in accordance with Aristotelian and scholastic terminology), continuing the ironic contrast between body and spirit introduced in the preceding stanza.

5   In Rome on the merry stage which among the people is called
    Fiano, I saw Cassandrino, with a lamp in his hand, forced to
    descend from the open air into a cave where clanking chains and
    a frightful and strange lament can be heard. Speaking bold words
    with a trembling voice, for trembling he extinguishes the torch. [2]

6   Not too differently did the knight of Rat City begin the infernal
    descent, except that he had no lighted lamp, which the mice don't
    need in order to see, nor indeed using threats, for in that undertak-
    ing he saw that threats were worthless, and even if he had wanted
    to use them, I believe that he would hardly have had enough
    breath for that.

7   Silently, in the company of many spirits, he descended the sub-
    terranean bottoms. Without dropping suddenly there the road
    leads to the darkest and deepest abysses. Dog Cerberus wasn't
    heard barking there, nor whips hissing, nor angry reptiles; boats
    were not seen, nor marshes, nor spirits waiting naked on the
    grass. [3]

8   Without any guardian was the entrance and perpetually open the
    way, which only with difficulty can ever be attempted by living
    beings. From its beginning it was naturally prepared for the use
    of the dead, and so there is no reason for others to stand in the
    way of one's descent into the dark kingdoms.

9   And although they have the means, [4] the dead feel no desire to
    get out of there, because once detached, the ego of the mouse
    does not attach itself again to the corporeal burden, and they
    know well that, returning from eternal oblivion, they would make

---

[2] Fiano was a famous theater of marionettes in Rome in Leopardi's
time, and Cassandrino, one of its comic characters, was created by Filippo
Teoli (1806-1844). His name derived from Cassandro of the Commedia dell'
arte.

[3] This is the traditional representation of the underworld of several
classical poets, including Virgil and Dante.

[4] This complacent attitude of the dead is very similar to that described
in one of the Operette morali, "Dialogue between Frederick Ruych and
his Mummies."

one's hair stand on end, and they would be shunned by everyone and cursed even by their close relatives.

10 The count found neither rewards nor punishments in the kingdom of the dead, at least his very ancient stories don't give any sign of it. And in this they don't surprise me, because, to tell the truth, wise Homer as well as ancient Israel never mentioned or rather never knew the dead to get what their life deserved, eternal pleasure or eternal pain.

11 Know that if this doctrine was for a long time thought to be found in him, [5] that happened because the human mind believes to be true not only those dogmas with which it was nourished as a child, but those of every people, however ancient or foreign. Just now we discovered that what Homer was reported to say about that was wrong: and this is called learning. [6]

12 Never did any savage have an inkling of rewards or punishments destined to the dead, nor indeed believe that after the death of the earthly limbs the souls live outside, but that the cold veins still pulsate and, in sum, that he who dies does not die; because one who is completely uncivilized and almost childlike is not capable of understanding death.

13 Therefore the savage believes that this fleeting and corporeal life, no other, and the brief human voyage continue forever after death in unknown ways and places, and that the buried also have the same state as they had above in their passage, [7] the same needs, and in no way changed the activities and the wealth.

14 And so he places underground with the lifeless remains food, riches, and clothes. He encloses the women and the servants, in order that the tomb may not deprive the deceased of his pleasures, dogs, arrows, and tools pertaining to whatever job he did, especially if destiny had prescribed that he procure his food with his hands.

---

[5] In Homer.

[6] That is, to learn is to dispel false beliefs.

[7] When they were alive.

15 And this is that universal consensus which with eloquence and vast knowledge is cited by very serious scholars as evidence of the future life of all the most uncouth and most feeble-minded peoples, of all the sluggish and uncultured minds: the incapacity to imagine in their deprived fantasy what death is.

16 Down there in the bottom are endless rows of seats which neither file nor chisel can cut into. The dead are sitting in every chair, their hands resting on little canes, the low-born and the noble mixed together as one by one the grave had them. As soon as one row is filled, the following one is occupied by the newcomers.

17 No one looks at his neighbor or speaks to him. If you have ever seen any paintings of the type done before Giotto, or ancient statues in some Gothic — as the ignorant [8] herd says — sepulcher, one of those which are frightening to look at, with their elongated and drowsy faces and their other members hanging and falling down,

18 imagine that the spirits down there in the other world have precisely such a form, and our heroic mouse found them to be like that when he had arrived at the very bottom. Up to that point he had trembled all the while during the descent — I don't conceal the truth — but when he saw that funereal chorus, he almost remained dead with them.

19 Perhaps with such, indeed not with so much horror you have seen Emperor Frederick the Second [9] in his flesh and in his clothes, lying in Palermo for six hundred years, without nose or lips and of that color which time can cause with its long ravages, but with his sword in his belt and his crown on his head and the image of the world at his side.

20 After the count had slowly and with great difficulty recovered from his fear, he got used to gazing into the half-closed eyes and

---

[8] Because that art which was called "Gothic" had nothing to do with the Goths.

[9] The body of Emperor Frederick II had been exhumed several years earlier (1781) in the Cathedral of Palermo.

at the faces of the ancient crowd, trying to see whether among them he could recognize from familiar features a friend. For a long time his eyes roamed, not recognizing anyone out of so many.

21   Everyone's appearance had so changed and they all looked so much alike that in the end he hardly recognized from the front Ham-Eater, Chunk-Stealer, and a few other holy souls of his dear friends recently killed. Addressing his discourse mainly to them, he told why he had undertaken to search for them.

22   But he had to begin from the crabs' first assault on his people, since to those descended to the bottom before that time what had happened afterwards was new. Indeed every day mice descend from the terrestrial slime to the world of the heroes, but they don't say a word, because to the dead this life up here is of no concern.

23   When he had told everything in detail — the truce, the new leader and the constitution, the ugly deceit of the enemies, and the ugly galloping of the bearded army [10] — he asked whether the shame and the grief into which the nation of the mice had fallen would be cleared away with the aid of the many allies recently assembled by him.

24   The deceased is not an animal who laughs. On the contrary, by eternal law he is denied the virtue by which it is given to the living when they discern an unusual stupidity to relieve with a loud and convulsive act an itching of the internal part. Therefore, when they heard the count's question, those departed to the other life did not laugh.

25   For the first time, however, a joyous sound spread upward through the perpetual night and from century to century reached the most remote caves as far as the bottom. The destinies trembled for fear that the laws imposed on the other world had been broken and that gloomy Elysium, [11] having heard the count, would not be able to contain its laughter.

---

[10] The army of the mice.
[11] The underground residence of the virtuous souls, the paradise of the Greeks and of the Romans.

26 The count, even though fear had control over his thoughts, having
    seen that ancient and modern times almost laughed at him and
    that the whole underworld, sweating, made a great effort to hold
    back the forbidden laughs, would have blushed, if by blushing
    mice could manifest their shame externally.

27 And confused and completely bewildered and with as humble a
    voice as possible, and in a still lowly and frightened posture,
    changing the form and style of his question, he consulted the
    spirits about the course of action a noble heart should follow in
    order to free his race of mice from the shame which covered it.

28 As a rusty and stiff lute which has remained silent for many years
    responds with a hoarse and obscure sound to one who tries it
    out or by chance strikes it, so with a turbid and impure utterance
    made partly with their lips and partly with their noses, breaking
    the ancient custom of silence, the shades answered the one
    from the outside world.

29 And they told him that, on seeing the sun again, he should find
    a way to go among his people, that since he could enter into the
    depth of the terrestrial mass, there too he could go. And there
    he should follow in thought, word, and deed what would be
    shown him to wash away the dishonor of his people by the general
    named Taster. [12]

30 This was a hoary and brave warrior who, valued and respected
    for his wisdom and virtue, fled the vain praise of vain ventures,
    living as much as possible in seclusion, leaving it to people of
    not very adult mind to prattle as though they were discussing
    serious matters, and, beneath a not splendid roof, loathing the
    grave look of servitude.

31 He happened to be lying ill when his people fled from the crab,
    and, invited to participate in theatrical conspiracies, he had closed

    _____

    [12] Although some critics have identified Taster with General Colletta,
    it is more likely that in this character Leopardi expressed his own ideas
    and feelings.

his ears from then on, and so at times he was called a bad citizen by the fugitive heroes, and he, calm in his virtue, laughed at the not very wise nature of others.

32 Having obtained such a prophecy, the count retraced his steps to the supernal regions bearing written in his gestures and on his face the terror of the infernal valleys. As once the people admitted into the caves of Trophonius to the mysteries of Styx and Acheron [13] returned, pale and transformed, upon the open shore.

33 Near the threshold of the narrow-mouthed cave he found Daedalus waiting for him, and after, discussing with him a bit what he had seen inside there, he had rested beneath that dark veil of fog which never lifts, with the wings readjusted on his back, in his company he again left the sand.

34 The half-dead one had the impression of coming to life again, when he came out of the darkness to see again the stars. [14] It was night and over the endless ocean the movable little lights were sparkling; the fleeting and nimble breezes gently whipped that shoreless sea, [15] and the rumble that the two made flying accompanied that sound.

35 So rapidly that it did not yield to the wind, they immediately directed their flight towards Rat City, keeping their eyes fixed on the two lights always at our pole. [16] In passing they discerned the liquid element strewn with islands, and over the dark ground owls flying, and more than one bat which drew close to the mouse as to a brother.

36 Having passed over the water, they passed over a great tract of dry land and then another sea, and just as they had done before

---

[13] The cavern of Trophonius was a cave of oracles situated in Boetia and, according to the legend, whoever descended into it returned pale with fear and remained forever sad.

[14] The famous line with which the thirty-fourth canto of Dante's *Inferno* ends.

[15] The sky.

[16] The Great Bear and the Little Bear.

they again passed over the region where we live. Already before them day was breaking and quickly spreading over the eastern mountains when Daedalus and the count lowered their wings near the rock of Rat City.

37   There, unseen, they restored their exhausted strength with berries and wild acorns. Then Daedalus, having gotten I don't know how in those parts a crab skin, covered the other with the enemy burden so that later on among the wicked beasts he seemed like a real crab, more real than among the French the bosoms and the hips of women seem. [17]

38   At last, wishing a propitious and successful outcome to the honorable enterprises of the count, the kind host, guide, and counselor, on going away, took his leave of him. [18] The mouse wept, and with his arms outstretched he swore him an eternally grateful heart. The other embraced him as well as he could, and then alone towards his nest he continued his flight.

39   The refugee did not defer re-entering the afflicted city, and after he had gone over it affectionately with his eyes and with his ears eagerly drunk in the native voices, without any delay he went straight to the one who he had heard could be a light to his people, I mean to the warrior of whom it is written above.

40   He introduced himself and revealed the desire which urged him to come. The other honored him highly, but he did not want to hear anything about plots or civil enterprises. The count tried to soften him up with prayers, but he did not mention the flight and the infernal country, because he was afraid of being taken for a visionary and a fool by that white-haired warrior.

41   Sometimes alone, sometimes in the company of others the inde-fatigable speaker had often returned to the attack and had not

---

[17] Reference to the fashion among French women to wear false bosoms and hips in order to accentuate their prominence.

[18] This farewell scene reproduces in a comic tone Virgil's farewell to Dante at the summit of Purgatorio.

opened any path to that heart. Finally, one day when with several young men at his side he was assailing Taster, the latter spoke to them in the manner which I had planned to narrate from here on.

42   Because, though the ancient parchments following which I have brought my story up to this point are lacking here and so the way was cut off to me, I hoped to find complete elsewhere in whatever learned language the legend contained therein: but the idea had no results, contrary to my wishes.

43   In Sanskrit language and Tibetan, in Hindustani, Pali and Japanese, Arabic, Rabbinic, Persian, Ethiopic, Tartar and Chinese, Syriac, Chaldean, Egyptian, Mesogothic, Saxon and Welsh, Finnish, Serbian and Dalmatian, Walachian, Provençal, Greek and Latin, this legend

44   lies hidden in many, many libraries of the East and of the West, which I myself checked and which were turned upside-down for me by more than one intelligent friend. But none of such writings buried there was of any use to my case, because there is not a single text of the legend which proceeds any further than ours.

45   Therefore with deep regret I am compelled to abandon my story here, cutting it short, since all of the texts are incomplete at the end, as I have said, whatever the reason may be: like a traveler who for lack of horses or wheels is forced to remain at the inn, or like a navigator intent on his course when the wind fails.

46   You, my readers, must not impute to me the involuntary incompletion. If I ever find complete in some book of legends what you have heard in part, I shall add an appendix to what I have narrated above, if you still want to read. Meanwhile be satisfied with the good intention, and let the eighth canto end here.

A SELECTED BIBLIOGRAPHY

I. ITALIAN EDITIONS OF THE *Paralipomena:*

On account of the strict censorship then prevailing in Italy, the first edition, the *Paralipomeni della Batracomiomachia di Giacomo Leopardi,* was published in Paris, in 1842, by the Libreria Europa di Baudry, Quais Malaquais, 3. The poem was printed by the press of Madame Lacombe with money advanced by F. P. Ruggiero in the name of A. Ranieri, who had entrusted the manuscript to him and had secured the printing through an acquaintance of his, Eugène Aroux, a French scholar interested in Italian literature. After 1845 Le Monnier of Florence made several reprints in which the errors of the original edition were increased rather than eliminated. Some editions worthy of mention, since the majority were modeled on that of Le Monnier in a more or less accurate manner, are those edited by G. Chiarini, *I Paralipomeni della Batracomiomachia di Giacomo Leopardi,* with notes by F. Ambrosoli (Leghorn: Vigo, 1869); by G. Mestica, *Opere approvate di Giacomo Leopardi* (Florence: Le Monnier, 1906); by A. Donati, *Versi, Paralipomeni della Batracomiomachia* (Bari: Laterza, 1921); and by E. Allodoli with a long introduction, *I Paralipomeni della Batracomiomachia* (Turin: U. T. E. T., 1921).

The standard critical edition of the *Paralipomena,* on which all successive editions as well as the present translation are based, is that of F. Moroncini, in *Opere minori approvate di Giacomo Leopardi,* Vol. I: *Poesie* (Bologna: L. Cappelli, 1931), which is preceded by an erudite introduction of great value.

Among the later editions that should be mentioned are those edited by G. De Robertis, in *Opere di Giacomo Leopardi,* Vol. I (Milan: Rizzoli, 1937); by F. Flora, in *Tutte le opere di Giacomo Leopardi,* Vol. I (Milan: Mondadori, 1940); by S. Solmi, with notes, in *Opere,* Tome I (Milan-Naples: Ricciardi, 1956); and by C. Muscetta and G. Savoca, *Canti, Paralipomeni, poesie varie, traduzioni poetiche e versi puerili* (Turin: Einaudi, 1968).

II. CRITICAL STUDIES IN ITALIAN ON THE *Paralipomena* AND ON LEOPARDI IN GENERAL:

On the *Paralipomena:*

Bacchelli, Renato. "I Paralipomeni della Batracomiomachia" and "Digressione sui Paralipomeni," in *Leopardi e Manzoni.* Milan: Mondadori, 1960.

Binni, Walter. *La nuova poetica leopardiana.* Florence: Sansoni, 1962. Chapt. XII. (first edition, 1947)
Boffito, Giuseppe. "Il 'Dedalo moderno' nei 'Paralipomeni' del Leopardi," *Giornale storico della letteratura italiana,* CXI (1938), pp. 76-85.
Brilli, Attilio. *Satira e mito nei Paralipomeni leopardiani.* Urbino: Argalia, 1968.
Capucci, Martino. "I *Paralipomeni* e la poetica leopardiana," *Convivium,* 22 (1954), pp. 581-594.
———. "La poesia dei *Paralipomeni* leopardiani," *Convivium,* 22 (1954), pp. 695-711.
Caserta, Ernesto. "Motivi poetici dominanti nei *Paralipomeni,*" *Revue des études italiennes,* XVII, n. 4 (1971), pp. 318-351.
Cassarà, Salvatore. *La politica del Leopardi nei Paralipomeni.* Palermo: Giannone e Lamantia, 1886.
Donadoni, Eugenio. "I *Paralipomeni* e le idee politiche di Giacomo Leopardi," in *Scritti e discorsi letterari.* Florence, 1921.
Levi, Giulio. "Capponi, Colletta e i *Paralipomeni della Batracomiomachia,*" *La Cultura,* 9 (1930), pp. 597-607.
Pasini, Ferdinando. "Umorismo leopardiano, i *Paralipomeni,*" *Annali della R. Università degli Studi Economici e Commerciali di Trieste,* IX (1937-38).
Pagnotti, Tommaso. *Il canto terzo dei Paralipomeni della Batracomiomachia di Giacomo Leopardi: Saggio di un commento nuovo.* Spoleto: Ragnoli, 1901.
Ramat, Silvio, "Vitalità dei *Paralipomeni,*" *Forum Italicum,* II, no. 2 (1968), pp. 95-101.
Savarese, Gennaro. *Saggio sui "Paralipomeni" di Giacomo Leopardi.* Florence: La Nuova Italia, 1967.

On Leopardi in general:

Battaglia, Salvatore. *Ideologia letteraria di Giacomo Leopardi.* Naples: Liguori, 1968.
Bigongiari, Pìero. *Leopardi.* Florence: Vallecchi, 1962.
Bosco, Umberto. *Titanismo e pietà in Giacomo Leopardi.* Florence: Le Monnier, 1957.
Cecchetti, Giovanni. *Leopardi e Verga.* Florence: La Nuova Italia, 1962.
Consoli, Domenico. *Cultura, coscienza letteraria e poesia in G. Leopardi.* Florence: Le Monnier, 1967.
Croce, Benedetto. "Leopardi," in *Poesia e non poesia.* Bari: Laterza, 1922.
De Robertis, Giuseppe. *Saggio sul Leopardi.* Florence: Vallecchi, 1952.
De Sanctis, Francesco. *Leopardi,* edited by C. Muscetta and A. Perna. Turin: Einaudi, 1960. (There are several editions of De Sanctis' essays.)
Frattini, Alberto. *Giacomo Leopardi.* Bologna: Cappelli, 1969.
Gentile, Giovanni. *Manzoni e Leopardi.* Milan: Treves, 1928.
Getto, Giovanni. *Saggi leopardiani.* Florence: Vallecchi, 1966.
Malagoli, Luigi. *Il grande Leopardi.* Florence: La Nuova Italia, 1960. (first edition, 1937)
Marzot, Giulio. *Storia del riso leopardiano.* Messina-Florence: D'Anna, 1966.
Ramat, Silvio. *Psicologia della forma leopardiana.* Florence: La Nuova Italia, 1970.
Sapegno, Natalino. *La poesia di Leopardi.* Rome, 1946.
Saponaro, Michele. *Leopardi.* Milan: Garzanti, 1941.

Solmi, Sergio. *Scritti leopardiani.* Milan: All'Insegna del pesce d'oro, 1969.
Vossler, Karl. *Leopardi.* Munich: Musarian Verlag, 1923. Ital. trans. by
T. Gnoli (Naples, 1925).

Due to the vast bibliography on Leopardi in Italian, we have had to
limit ours to the minimum. The reader wishing to continue his study
of Leopardi may consult the bibliographical work of G. Mazzantini, M. Men-
ghini, Giulio Natali, and G. Musumarra, *Bibliografia leopardiana,* in 3 vols.
(Florence: Olschki, 1931-51), and Alessandro Tortoreto, *Bibliografia anali-
tica leopardiana 1952-60* (Florence: Olschki, 1963). Also, the work of
P. Mazzamuto, *Rassegna bibliografico-critica della letteratura italiana,* 3rd ed.
(Florence: Le Monnier, 1963), is very useful. For the history of Leopardi
criticism, see:

Bigi, E. "Giacomo Leopardi," in *I classici italiani nella storia della critica,*
   edited by W. Binni, Vol. II. Florence: La Nuova Italia, 1955. Pp. 393-
   448.
Goffis, C. *Leopardi.* Palermo: Palumbo, 1961.
Giannessi, F. *La critica leopardiana.* Milan: La Goliardica, 1958, and Giannessi's essay in *Letteratura italiana, I maggiori,* Vol. II. Milan: Mar-
   zorati, 1956.
Frattini, A. *Saggio di una storia della critica e della fortuna dei Canti di
   G. Leopardi.* Brescia: La Scuola, 1958.

III. LEOPARDI IN ENGLISH:

Translations:

Giacomo Leopardi: Selected Prose and Poetry, edited, translated, and intro-
   duced by I. Origo and J. H. Stubbs. New York: The New American
   Library, 1966.
Leopardi's Canti Translated into English Verse, edited by J. H. Whitfield.
   Naples, 1962.
Leopardi: Poems and Prose, edited by A. Flores with an introduction by
   S. Pacifici. Bloomington: Indiana University Press, 1966.
The Penguin Book of Italian Verse, edited by George R. Kay. Baltimore:
   Penguin Books, 1966. (first edition, 1958)

Studies:

Origo, Iris. *Leopardi: A Study in Solitude.* London: H. Hamilton, 1953.
Perella, Nicola J. *Night and the Sublime in Giacomo Leopardi.* Berkeley-
   Los Angeles-London: University of California Press, 1970.
Singh, Ghan. *Leopardi and the Theory of Poetry.* Lexington: University of
   Kentucky Press, 1964.
Whitfield, John H. *Giacomo Leopardi.* Oxford: Blackwell, 1954.

For an almost complete bibliography of studies on Leopardi in English
both in England and in America, see: Singh, G. *Leopardi e l'Inghilterra.*
Florence: Le Monnier, 1968, pp. 202-214.

NORTH CAROLINA STUDIES IN THE
ROMANCE LANGUAGES AND LITERATURES

I.S.B.N. Prefix 0-88438

Recent Titles

FROM VULGAR LATIN TO OLD PROVENÇAL, by Frede Jensen. 1972. (No. 120). *-920-0*.

GOLDEN AGE DRAMA IN SPAIN: GENERAL CONSIDERATION AND UNUSUAL FEATURES, by Sturgis E. Leavitt. 1972. (No. 121). *-921-9*.

THE LEGEND OF THE "SIETE INFANTES DE LARA" (*Refundición toledana de la crónica de 1344* versión), study and edition by Thomas A. Lathrop. 1972. (No. 122). *-922-7*.

STRUCTURE AND IDEOLOGY IN BOIARDO'S "ORLANDO INNAMORATO," by Andrea di Tommaso. 1972. (No. 123). *-923-5*.

STUDIES IN HONOR OF ALFRED G. ENGSTROM, edited by Robert T. Cargo and Emmanuel J. Mickel, Jr. 1972. (No. 124). *-924-3*.

A CRITICAL EDITION WITH INTRODUCTION AND NOTES OF GIL VICENTE'S "FLORESTA DE ENGANOS," by Constantine Christopher Stathatos. 1972. (No. 125). *-925-1*.

LI ROMANS DE WITASSE LE MOINE. *Roman du treizième siècle.* Édité d'après le manuscrit, fonds français 1553, de la Bibliothèque Nationale, Paris, par Denis Joseph Conlon. 1972. (No. 126). *-926-X*.

EL CRONISTA PEDRO DE ESCAVIAS. *Una vida del Siglo XV,* por Juan Bautista Avalle-Arce. 1972. (No. 127). *-927-8*.

AN EDITION OF THE FIRST ITALIAN TRANSLATION OF THE "CELESTINA," by Kathleen V. Kish. 1973. (No. 128). *-928-6*.

MOLIÈRE MOCKED. THREE CONTEMPORARY HOSTILE COMEDIES: *Zélinde, Le portrait du peintre, Élomire Hypocondre,* by Frederick Wright Vogler. 1973. (No. 129). *-929-4*.

C.-A. SAINTE-BEUVE. *Chateaubriand et son groupe littéraire sous l'empire.* Index alphabétique et analytique établi par Lorin A. Uffenbeck. 1973. (No. 130). *-930-8*.

THE ORIGINS OF THE BAROQUE CONCEPT OF "PEREGRINATIO," by Juergen Hahn. 1973. (No. 131). *-931-6*.

THE "AUTO SACRAMENTAL" AND THE PARABLE IN SPANISH GOLDEN AGE LITERATURE, by Donald Thaddeus Dietz. 1973. (No. 132). *-932-4*.

FRANCISCO DE OSUNA AND THE SPIRIT OF THE LETTER, by Laura Calvert. 1973. (No. 133). *-933-2*.

ITINERARIO DI AMORE: DIALETTICA DI AMORE E MORTE NELLA VITA NUOVA, by Margherita de Bonfils Templer. 1973. (No. 134). *-934-0*.

L'IMAGINATION POETIQUE CHEZ DU BARTAS: ELEMENTS DE SENSIBILITE BAROQUE DANS LA "CREATION DU MONDE," by Bruno Braunrot. 1973. (No. 135). *-934-0*.

ARTUS DESIRE: PRIEST AND PAMPHLETEER OF THE SIXTEENTH CENTURY, by Frank S. Giese. 1973. (No. 136). *-936-7*.

JARDIN DE NOBLES DONZELLAS, FRAY MARTIN DE CORDOBA, by Harriet Goldberg. 1974. (No. 137). *-937-5*.

Symposia

LOS NARRADORES HISPANOAMERICANOS DE HOY, edited by Juan Bautista Avalle-Arce. 1973. (No. 1). *-951-0*.

When ordering please cite the *ISBN Prefix* plus the last four digits for each title.

Send orders to:

> University of North Carolina Press
> Chapel Hill
> North Carolina 27514
> U. S. A.

The Department of Romance Studies Digital Arts and Collaboration Lab at the University of North Carolina at Chapel Hill is proud to support the digitization of the North Carolina Studies in the Romance Languages and Literatures series.

DEPARTMENT OF
Romance Studies
Digital Arts and Collaboration Lab